MW01147707

Cowboy
Hearts

Cat Johnson

A CAT JOHNSON RED IMPRINT TITLE

PROLOGUE

Twelve years ago

"Dakota Washburn?"

"Here." Dakota nodded his dark head and answered from the desk in the row directly next to Justus.

"Justus White?" With her glasses riding so low on her nose that Justus feared they'd fall off, the teacher continued to read off the attendance list.

"Here." Justus held his breath and waited, knowing after hearing this list read in the same order every school day since last September, whose name came right after his.

"And finally, Melody Zaine." The teacher glanced up from the paper in her hand.

"Here." Her long, straight brown hair flowing over her shoulders, Melody raised her perfect arm into the air, her voice as sweet and beautiful as her name as she answered.

Mrs. Stowe took off her glasses and put them down on her desk, along with the attendance list.

"All right then, everyone's here. That's wonderful since today, as you know, is Valentine's Day. Did everyone bring in their valentines?" The room full of ten-year-olds nodded. "Good, so here is how it's going to work. When I call your row, everyone seated in that row will get up in an orderly manner and put their valentines into the mailboxes on each student's desk. Okay? We'll start with the front row first."

Of course she started with the front row first. Teachers always started in the front. Justus, having a last name that started with a W, was in the last row, as usual. He leaned back and prepared to wait forever for his turn, like he'd been doing since kindergarten.

Dakota reached across the distance between them and poked Justus in the left elbow. "I bet I get more than you."

Justus scowled. "More what? Valentine cards? You can't get more than me. The teacher said we have to give one to everybody in the class."

"Yeah, well, maybe I'll get an extra one. A special one." Dakota shot a meaningful glance at Melody, seated to Justus's right. "Maybe from someone who keeps looking at me like she likes me."

"Whatever." As a sense of horror hit him, Justus tried to act like it didn't matter, but it did. He liked Melody. She couldn't like Dakota instead of him. Besides, Melody had been talking an extra lot to Justus lately. She'd even shared her cookies with him just yesterday during lunch.

Justus was barely aware of his own cardboard shoebox he'd made into a mailbox even though it was quickly filling with small colored envelopes covered in scrawling letters that spelled out his name.

Only one valentine would matter to him. Hers. Just like only one of the twenty-five he'd written out until his hand had cramped last night really mattered to him.

Hers.

"Okay, now students in row number two." From her seat at the big desk in the front of the room, Mrs. Stowe continued to direct the Valentine's Day traffic of children winding their way, row by row, through the classroom.

Justus clutched the envelope meant for Melody in his hand. He'd done the bravest thing ever. He'd signed it "Love, Justus." On all the other cards, he'd just put his name. He could only hope Melody realized that and what it meant.

Once again he cursed the fact that he and Melody both were in the last row. He wanted to deliver his envelope and his declaration of love to her already. Then after he did, by the time he got back to his desk, hers would be in his mailbox. Should he open his valentine from her then and there? Or wait until lunchtime?

Nope, no way he could wait.

But then he glanced sideways and realized he couldn't open it here either. Not with nosey Dakota sitting just a few feet away.

An idea hit Justus. He'd slip the envelope into his pocket and tell the teacher he had to go to the bathroom. Then he could open it in private. But how would he know which one was hers unless he opened all of them and looked?

He frowned. This love stuff was complicated, but it would be worth it if Melody liked—no, not liked, *loved* him, too. He'd have to wait and see. Maybe Mrs. Stowe would tell them when they were allowed to open the cards.

After what seemed like a year, Mrs. Stowe finally said, "Okay, the students in the back row may deliver their valentines."

Stifling his whoop of excitement, Justus jumped up, and then remembered he needed to deliver all of his valentines, not just Melody's. He reached beneath the lid of his desk and grabbed the stack, but the first one he delivered was to her, shoving it into the mailbox's top hole, which she had cut out with scissors and decorated with red glitter and crayon hearts.

Justus tapped the top of the box just to make sure it stayed in there, nice and safe, so it didn't get lost. Then, with a backward glance at the box on her desk that contained his declaration of love, he moved to the next row and started to distribute the rest.

In record time, Justus was done with the delivery and crawling into his desk chair. Somehow Dakota had beaten him back to his desk. He sat grinning from ear to ear.

Justus frowned. "What are you smiling about?"

"A secret." Dakota's grin widened.

Justus noticed Dakota held a valentine in his hand. It was out of the envelope and open. "Mrs. Stowe didn't say we could open any yet."

Dakota shrugged. "So. She can't see way back here. Why? You gonna tattle on me?"

"No." Justus screwed up his mouth in a pout.

Not that he wouldn't love to because he had a very bad suspicion the valentine that had Dakota so happy was from Melody. Now he itched even more to find his from her. But he wasn't the kind of kid who broke the rules, unlike Dakota, obviously.

Practically bouncing in his chair, Justus eyed Mrs. Stowe at her desk. She sat perfectly calmly, thanking each student as they delivered her their cards.

Finally everyone had taken his or her seats again and Mrs. Stowe stood. "All right, class. Open your valentines."

Justus tore into his mailbox, sacrificing the red paper he'd wrapped it in when Mrs. Stowe had forced them all to decorate their shoeboxes. His was actually made from a boot box since that's what his mom had at their house. That meant it had even more room for him to paw through looking for the envelope that was most likely to contain Melody's valentine to him.

He shot a look at the torn envelope on Dakota's desk— the one he suspected was from her—and saw it was white with red writing on it.

That was a clue.

Justus flung any colored envelopes aside and focused on the white ones with red writing. One stood out from the rest. It had a little red heart drawn next to his name.

With his own heart pounding, Justus tore into the valentine.

She'd made it by hand by cutting a heart out of red construction paper and gluing gold glitter onto the outside.

With a glance at Dakota to make sure he was busy with his own mailbox, Justus opened the card.

Her letters spelled out his name, and under that she'd

written, *meet me in the woods behind the monkey bars during recess for a kiss.*

Holy cow!

Shaking at just the thought of meeting Melody alone, Justus forced himself to remain calm and glanced at Dakota. He sat, still looking smug, but this time Justus wasn't jealous. Dakota may have gotten a valentine from Melody, but Justus was sure it didn't contain that extra special message from her like his did.

Not just any message, but an invitation.

An invitation to meet her in the woods for a kiss.

His heart pounded harder as he glanced at the clock. There were thirty whole minutes to go before recess. How could he stand to wait? He wanted to go now because today was going to be very, very special.

Today, he'd get his very first kiss.

~ * ~

Dakota ran directly for the monkey bars the moment Mrs. Stowe said they could go to recess. He didn't stop at his locker for his jacket like Justus and the rest of the class did, which is why he got outside long before all the other kids.

That was his plan. He wanted to be there, waiting for Melody when she arrived. And he certainly didn't want Justus tagging along with him. Not today. Not to meet her.

Ever since he'd hidden the Valentine she'd given him beneath his desk and read what she'd written, he'd been planning how to get here to the woods to meet her without anyone else seeing.

As he started to shiver in the cold Colorado air, he decided freezing would be worth it just to spend time with her alone. Even if he did catch pneumonia from being outside without a coat, like his mother always warned, he wouldn't care. One kiss from Melody would cure him.

And getting a kiss from Melody, when he knew Justus liked her too, would be even better. Dakota liked to win.

"Hi."

Dakota had been so busy imagining her arrival, and

pretending he wasn't shaking from the cold, he'd missed that she'd walked up and was standing not far from him now.

He smiled even as his teeth chattered. "Hi."

Melody's brows crinkled above her chocolate-colored eyes. "Where's your coat?"

He shrugged. "I don't need a coat. I hardly ever wear one."

"Oh."

Was she impressed at how tough he was? Dakota hoped so. He was about to take a step forward, say something clever and then lean in for a kiss, when Justus came crashing across the trampled snow. His wool hat was pulled so low over his forehead that it totally covered all of his light-colored hair.

Justus frowned and stared right at Dakota. "What are you doing here? And where's your coat?"

Justus was bundled up in not only a ski hat and jacket, but in a scarf and gloves, too. Had Justus's mommy come to school and dressed him for recess? That's the only reason to wear all that stuff when your mother couldn't see you.

Dakota shook his head. "I don't need it. And what are you doing here?"

Justus hooked a gloved thumb in Melody's direction. "She invited me."

"She couldn't have." Dakota frowned. "She invited me."

Melody, looking really cute in her pink leopard coat, took a step forward, putting herself between him and Justus. "I invited both of you."

Dakota stared at her. "Why?"

"I'm not sure which one of you I like better."

"So you invited us both here? What are you going to do? Kiss us both?" Justus looked as shocked as Dakota felt.

"Uh, huh. I'm going to kiss you both and see which one I like better."

"All right." Dakota guessed he could live with that. Since he'd kissed Susan O'Shea last year, at least he had some experience over Justus in this area. "Me first."

Justus let out a snort. "No. Why do you get to go first?"

"Because I called it." Dakota took a step closer to Melody, which also put him closer to Justus.

"Calling it doesn't count." Justus moved forward until they were nearly chest-to-chest.

"Sure it does. Besides, I know how to kiss a girl. You don't." Dakota poked Justus in the chest to reinforce his point, not that Justus would be able to feel anything through all the thick padding of his coat.

"I do too. And don't poke me." With two hands, Justus shoved Dakota hard, sending him stumbling back.

Dakota tripped backward. He landed on his butt hard, but his pride hurt way worse than his cold, wet rear end.

Anger seethed through him. He scrambled to his feet and lurched at Justus.

The force knocked Justus to the ground with Dakota on top of him, fists flailing.

The two rolled. Dakota tried to punch him, but Justus was too fluffy from all the sissy snow gear he was wrapped in. Dakota couldn't land a decent shot anywhere that would hurt.

Meanwhile Justus, who fought like a girl, had a handful of Dakota's hair clenched in his fist, yanking at it hard.

"Boys! Stop that!"

Mrs. Stowe and half the class were standing nearby when Dakota looked up. "Tell him to let go of my hair."

Justus still held tight. "Only if you stop punching me."

"Fine." Dakota's hands were starting to hurt from the cold anyway.

"Dakota. Where is your coat?" Mrs. Stowe brushed the snow off both of them once they finally stood.

What was it with everyone and his coat? Dakota shrugged. "In my locker."

Mrs. Stowe shook her head. "Inside now. Both of you. The rest of you go back to recess."

As he shoved his numb fingers into the front pockets of his jeans, Dakota glanced at Melody. She stood by, a wide smile on her face.

Walking next to him out of the woods, Justus glanced

sideways. "She wanted us to fight."

"Mrs. Stowe?" Dakota frowned.

"No, idiot. Melody. She enjoyed it. She was smiling. Melody invited us both here at the same time so we'd fight over her."

"You think?" Dakota asked.

"Sure. If she just wanted to kiss us both like she said, she could have invited us at different times and to different places. Instead, she made sure we were both here at the same place and at the same time."

Though Dakota hated to admit Justus was right about anything, what he said did make sense. "Why would she want us to fight over her?"

Justus shrugged. "Because girls are idiots."

If Melody had planned this just so she could get two guys to fight over her, Dakota had a better word for her than idiot. It started with a B and rhymed with *witch*.

Meanwhile, he was very aware that every student on the playground was staring and whispering about them. That made him even angrier than he'd been before.

Dakota glanced sideways at Justus. "I'm sorry I punched you."

Justus turned his head to look at him as they both plodded toward the door of the building. "I'm sorry I pushed you and pulled your hair."

"Yeah, about that." Dakota shook his head. "Dude, you need to learn how to fight better."

"Hey! I know how to fight."

"Yeah, whatever." Dakota laughed. "You know, my brother teaches MMA."

"Mixed martial arts? Really?" Justus looked impressed.

"Yup. He shows me a lot of stuff." Proud, Dakota stood a bit straighter. "Like he taught me how to throw a good punch. If you come over after school, I can show you what he showed me if you want."

"Okay, I guess."

Dakota, feeling the cold even more now that his clothes

were wet and the excitement of the fight was subsiding, glanced at Justus again. "Friends?"

"Yeah. Friends. But let's make a pact. We'll never let a girl get between us again. Deal?" Justus reached out and pulled open the door. He held it as Dakota walked through.

Inside the blessed warmth of the school, Dakota nodded. "Deal."

CHAPTER ONE

Justus took a sip of his beer as he watched Dakota bend low over the pool table and line up his shot. There was the crack of balls hitting one another and the felt bumpers as the striped ball he'd aimed at sunk into the corner pocket, followed by the cue ball.

"Crap." Dakota turned away from the table, scowling. "You're up."

"Yes, I am. Watch and weep, sucker." Justus grinned. Reaching for the cue ball in the ball return, he put it back on the table in line with the eight ball. He sunk the black ball easily and straightened up to glance at Dakota. "That's the game. This round is on you."

"Yeah, yeah. I know. I'll be right back." Dakota reached for his wallet in his back pocket and turned toward the bar.

Justus smiled and raised the long neck to his lips again. He loved nothing more than beating Dakota. The next beer, bought with his friend's money instead of his own, would taste even better than this one did.

"Justus!"

He glanced up when Dakota called his name from the bar. "Yeah?"

"They're out of bottles. Draft okay?"

"Sure." Beer was beer. In fact, Justus figured a person would be hard pressed to find a twenty-two-year-old who was picky about what he drank, especially when someone else was buying.

"Justus? I thought that was you. Hey there." The soft feminine voice had Justus turning.

He knit his brows in a frown as the brunette stepped out of the shadows and into the light of the lamp suspended above the pool table. It took him a second but then it hit him—memories of grade school and her. "Melody?"

Smiling, she nodded. "I'm surprised you remember me."

Ha! How could he forget? It was her he had thought about every day of fifth grade. His ten-year-old self had such a crush on her until her family had moved away. Even after that Valentine's Day where he realized she was only playing him and Dakota, he was still devastated when she'd left at the end of the school year.

"What are you doing back here? Didn't you move to Denver?" He dropped his gaze briefly to her chest, which had definitely grown since fifth grade, before he dragged his focus back up to her face.

"We did. My parents are still there. I'm here visiting my grandparents."

Her hair was shorter, hitting her shoulder rather than touching her waist the way it had in school when he'd stared at her whenever he could without her noticing.

It was amazing he'd passed that grade, given how much time and thought he'd given to Melody rather than his schoolwork.

Justus was paying so much attention to Melody now, he didn't notice Dakota until he thrust a beer mug into his line of sight and asked, "Who's this?"

Dakota hadn't recognized her. Justus's instinct to be jealous began to kick in before he squashed it.

"Dakota?" Melody laughed. "Wow. You guys are still friends? That's great."

Looking confused, Dakota frowned. After a few seconds, realization dawned and his eyes opened wide. "Melody? You're back."

He shot a sideways look at Justus.

Justus knew they were both remembering the same thing—their fight in the woods behind the monkey bars.

"She's back for a visit with her grandparents."

"Ah." Dakota nodded.

The players may be the same, but things were very different now. Mainly, he and Dakota were twenty-two-year-old men, not ten-year-old boys. They lived and worked together, twenty-four hours a day, seven days a week, at the Maverick ranch.

They were best friends. More than that, they'd begun to train and compete together as team ropers, so they were partners too.

Twelve years ago they'd vowed to never let a girl get in the way of their friendship, and now the girl who'd caused them to make that promise stood before them.

Justus glanced at Dakota, trying to judge if they were still on the same page in that respect. Dakota liked the ladies well enough. Hell, so did Justus. But this particular one had spelled trouble for them both.

Though that had been a long time ago. People changed. Had Melody?

"So how long you here for?" Dakota took a step closer to where Justus stood. He leaned his ass against the edge of the pool table so they were shoulder to shoulder, facing her opposite them.

Was that move meant to show Melody it was the boys against the girls? Maybe things hadn't changed all that much since fifth grade.

Then again, maybe Dakota's new boots hurt his feet and he needed to lean against something.

Matters involving females were just as confusing to Justus now as they had been then. Sad but true.

He needed to get out more.

"Just for the week, but if things work out, there's a chance I might be moving back." Melody eyed their mugs. "That beer looks nice and cold."

That was a hint if ever Justus heard one. He lifted a brow as he waited to see how Dakota would react.

Dakota took a sip and nodded slowly. "Yup. It sure is. You should get yourself one."

Melody's eyes widened and Justus had to restrain a smile at her obvious surprise.

Apparently, Dakota was still pissed about what she'd done all those years ago. They had gotten in some pretty big trouble for fighting. Their parents had been notified, so they'd both been grounded. And then for the rest of the month the two of them had to sit inside the classroom alone during recess and do schoolwork while the others in the class played outside.

All that punishment had done was seal their friendship. They grew closer from spending all that time together.

But once the rumor had spread they were fighting over Melody, she got even more popular, while Justus and Dakota got nothing but teased about it.

Come to think of it, Dakota probably had a right to be pissed off. Hell, if Justus wasn't such a forgiving person, he might still be mad too.

Melody, in the meantime, had pasted a sweet smile on her face. If she was shocked that the two cowboys she'd played so easily twelve years ago weren't going to jump to buy her a beer now, she'd hidden it.

"So do you two still live with your parents?"

Ouch.

There was a dig in that question and he knew it had nothing to do with the fact Dakota's parents had moved to Arizona and Justus's his mom had gone to live in Georgia with her sister after his dad had died.

She likely didn't know any of that. She was trying to insult them.

He'd heard a rumor she'd gone to college. She was

probably insinuating two cowboys with no more than a high school diploma couldn't make enough at whatever they did for a living to afford to move out.

Justus shook his head. "Nope. We both moved out years ago."

"Oh? You've got your own places." Her brows rose.

"We both live at the Maverick ranch." Dakota delivered that piece of news with a cocky smile.

In these parts, hell anywhere really, the name Maverick commanded a lot of respect. Old Jake Maverick may no longer be around, but the retail corporation his family had founded a hundred years ago, and the four-thousand-acre cattle ranch that had been in his family for generations, were household names.

Growing up, Justus could remember sitting in his father's truck and passing the big gates over the ranch entrance that read *Maverick*. Back then, Justus had never dreamed he'd ever work there, or actually live there, right along with the Maverick family.

Pride swelled in his chest. "We don't just live there. We work there, too, as ranch hands. Blue Boyd's our boss."

"Bonner Blue Boyd, the state rodeo champion?" Her eyes opened wider.

Ha! Score one for the cowboys. Whether she wanted to be or not, she was obviously impressed they knew Blue so well.

Justus nodded. "Yup."

"Well, I see I was wrong about you two." Melody crossed her arms over her chest.

"Wrong about what?" A deep frown creased Dakota's forehead.

She shrugged. "I'd assumed you'd never amount to anything. Ranch hands, impressive."

Justus didn't know much about a lot of things, but he knew sarcasm when he heard it. She was making fun of them. His insides steamed.

"Dakota, we probably should be getting home soon." Justus glanced at Dakota, and then swung his gaze back to

Melody. "The live-in housekeeper has breakfast on the dining room table for us at dawn every morning. She gets mighty pissed if we're late."

"That's right. And besides that, with Blue still away in New York handling stuff at Maverick Western corporate headquarters, we're in charge of the whole operation here. It's only four-hundred head, but we're nearing calving season, so there's a lot more to worry about." Dakota, quick as a whip, caught right on to Justus's plan and added more information that would hopefully fuel Melody's envy.

The best part was, not a word of it was a lie. They might sleep in the bunkhouse, but they did get to eat three meals a day, served to them by Mrs. Jones in the Maverick homestead's dining room. On holidays they even ate with the good silver. And with Blue away they really were in charge of the whole place.

Blue kept talking about hiring a ranch manager to run things when he was traveling, but he never seemed to get around to doing it.

Justus nudged Dakota in the side with his elbow as he thought of more to say to impress Melody. "Oh, and you know what else? We still have to email Miss Casey the changes we made to the agenda for that executive retreat she's planning to hold at the ranch next month."

"You're right." Dakota glanced at Melody. "Miss Casey is Maverick Western's director of marketing. When Mr. Maverick hired her for the New York headquarters last year, Justus and I had to take her around and show her ranch life and stuff. Now she wants us to help with this big training thing next month for the other managers and directors and stuff from New York."

That was kind of a stretch since it had been Blue who'd been assigned to show Miss Casey around, but they were right there working with him, so it was close enough to the truth.

Justus glanced at Melody and saw an odd expression on her face. Maybe she was starting to realize they weren't such dumb hicks after all. He smothered his smile at that and said, "So, Melody, what are you doing with yourself nowadays? You working? Going to school?"

"Well, um, I graduated from college."

"Congratulations." Dakota managed to be gracious.

Meanwhile, all Justus could think was *aw, crap*. She had a college degree. No wonder she was acting all superior.

"Yeah, thanks." Melody kicked the toe of her boot against the dingy bar floor and didn't make eye contact with him, which made Justus think there was more here than met the eye.

He decided to pursue it. "So you must have a really great job then. Right?"

"Not exactly." For the first time tonight, Melody looked human, with all the insecurities the rest of them had.

Gone was Miss Perfect with the superior attitude. Cracking through the uppity façade she'd put on since walking in here was what he suspected was the real Melody, the person she was when she wasn't putting on a show for everyone.

"Oh? What's up?" Justus asked.

"It's a really bad economy. And in hindsight, getting a degree in art history probably wasn't the smartest thing to do." She finally raised her gaze from the floor. "I'm having trouble finding a job. I've been looking since I graduated last May."

Today was February first. That was a long time to be without work. Justus had started working part time when he was fifteen and hadn't been without employment since. He couldn't even imagine what Melody was feeling.

He glanced at Dakota. Even he looked like he had softened a little bit toward her as well.

Justus turned back to Melody. "I'm sorry to hear that."

"I'm sure you'll find one eventually," Dakota added.

"Yeah. Eventually. That's why I'm here actually. There's an opening at our old school for a teacher. I have an interview. Can you imagine if I get the job? Me teaching fifth grade." She smiled and this time, it looked genuine.

"You'll be a huge improvement over old Mrs. Stowe," Justus said with a grin.

Melody laughed. "The sad thing is, *old* Mrs. Stowe was probably only like thirty-something when she taught us."

"Could be," Justus agreed, remembering their teacher's signature ugly sweaters. She had a different one for each holiday. "She's still there, you know, but she's assistant principal now."

"Yeah, that's what I heard," Melody said.

"Hey, you want a beer?" Justus was aware of the look Dakota shot him at that offer.

She smiled. "I'd love one. Thank you."

"Be right back." Justus pushed off the pool table, and tried to ignore Dakota's glare.

"I'll come with you." Dakota launched himself after Justus, and the moment they were out of earshot he poked him in the side. "Justus, what the hell are you doing?"

"Buying an old school friend a drink." Justus kept walking toward the bar.

"She hasn't changed." Dakota's tone let Justus know he wasn't happy with this new turn of events.

"One draft please." Justus leaned an elbow on the bar and turned toward Dakota. "I don't know. She seems a little bit more humble now that she has a fancy college degree and still can't find a job."

"And that'll change once she does get one. Then she'll be playing her little games with us again, just like she did back in Mrs. Stowe's class. What are you going to do then? Buy her another beer?" Dakota's expression turned hard.

After digging his wallet out of his pocket, Justus threw a five-dollar bill to the bartender. "No, I'm not. No girl comes between our friendship again. Remember?"

Dakota's brows rose. "Oh, I remember. It's your memory I'm worried about."

"Well, stop worrying. Kill them with kindness. That's what my gramps always used to say." He waved away his change from the bartender and grabbed the foam-filled mug off the bar.

"Let's hope your kindness doesn't kill our friendship. I'm going to take a piss." Dakota turned and stalked toward the restrooms in the back as Justus sighed.

Yup. Women sure did complicate things.

CHAPTER TWO

From the rear of the dimly lit bar, Dakota watched Justus standing close to Melody as she sipped on her beer—the beer Justus had bought her. She seemed to be drinking it in the most seductive way possible.

How could Justus not see she was the same girl she had been way back then? She'd probably be happy to see them rolling around on the beer-splattered floor fighting over her while the rest of the folks in the bar cheered them on.

She'd probably be wearing a big old grin the entire time, just like she'd done in fifth grade when she'd orchestrated their first and only fight.

Well he, for one, was not going to allow it to happen, no matter what Justus said or did.

Scowling, Dakota walked back to the pool table.

Justus glanced up and his smile disappeared. He must have caught on to Dakota's unhappiness. He turned back to Melody and hooked a thumb in the direction of the restrooms. "Ah, Melody, I'll be back in a sec. Okay?"

"Sure." She smiled sweetly.

As he moved close to Dakota, Justus leaned close and hissed, "Stop looking so pissed off."

Dakota's eyebrows shot up. "Then you stop acting as if she's changed."

"Maybe she has."

"Yeah, right." Dakota let out a snort.

"Whatever. Try and be nice while I'm gone." Justus let out a huff of breath and pushed past Dakota, heading back to the bathrooms.

"*Whatever*," Dakota mimicked Justus after he'd walked away.

That had to be the most annoying word in the English language, and the fact his best friend was saying it to him in such a nasty tone was proof that Melody was trouble.

Nothing but trouble.

Luckily, Dakota was good at dealing with problems. Hell, he dealt with difficult issues all damn day, and sometimes all night, at the ranch. Compared to stubborn young bulls and a couple of hundred cows about to give birth, one stuck-up chick shouldn't be too hard to handle.

Dakota made his way back to where he'd left his beer on the table and picked up the mug.

Taking a swallow, he leaned against the pool table again—his new going-out boots weren't broken in yet and they were starting to pinch.

"So, you're back and looking for work," he said to her.

They'd covered this topic already, but Dakota enjoyed it so much the first time, he decided to revisit the subject.

"You don't like me very much, do you, Dakota?"

"Nope." He shook his head and sipped his beer.

She laughed. "At least you're honest about it."

"I'm always honest, which is more than you were when you invited Justus and I to fight over you in front of the whole fifth grade."

"I can't believe you're actually still upset over something that happened in fifth grade. And I was being honest back then. I really didn't know which one of you I liked best."

"So you thought you'd see which one of us could beat the crap out of the other? Then what? You'd suddenly like the winner best? Nice."

"No." Her dark brows knit in a frown. "I really wanted to kiss you both. You two are the ones who started fighting. I never wanted that."

"Bullshit. You smiled through the whole thing." He knocked the bill of his ball cap back a bit so he could better glare at her.

"Because I couldn't believe you both liked me enough to fight over me." She put her mug down on the table with a splash and planted her fists on her hips.

"You're right. Fifth grade is long gone. That shit doesn't matter now." He made direct eye contact with her to make sure she knew he was serious. "But I'm telling you one thing—Justus and I are closer than brothers now. We're not ten years old any more and we sure as hell ain't gonna be fighting over you again. So if you've got any ideas in your pretty little head about pitting us against each other in some sort of competition for you, you can just forget about it."

Movement caught his eye and he turned to see Justus standing nearby, watching them. Dakota spun to face him, silently daring him to contradict what he'd said.

"Dakota's right, Melody. He and I aren't going to be fighting over anything." Justus swung his glance from Melody to Dakota. "But I'm sure Melody has more weighing on her mind right now. Her interview for one thing. She won't have time to be worrying about us. Right?"

"Right," she agreed.

Dakota's gaze moved between Justus and Melody. "That's fine, but I needed to set things straight, right up front so there's no doubt in anybody's mind how things stand."

"I understand just fine," Melody snorted. "And don't you worry because I have a boyfriend."

"Oh?" Justus swatted him in the ribs. "See, Dakota. She has a boyfriend."

Yeah, sure. And Dakota had a million dollars buried under the bunkhouse.

Bullshit.

He knew a lie when he heard it. Damn girl had better never play poker because she couldn't bluff for crap. "Uh, huh. That's nice. What's his name?"

"Bob." There had been the briefest hesitation before Melody answered, during which she got a look of panic on her face.

Dakota stood by his theory that she was lying. "Bob, huh? And what does Bob do for a living?"

"He's a, uh, attorney."

"Attorney? Wow. That's impressive. How old is he?"

"He's my age. Well maybe he's a year older."

She didn't know how old her boyfriend was? She was totally lying. Dakota smiled. "Hmm, that's extra impressive since attorneys have to go to regular college for four years then to law school for three years, and then take the bar exam. He must be really smart. Did he graduate high school at like fourteen?"

Melody's eyes narrowed. "Okay, fine. There is no Bob."

Justus spun to her with a frown. "Then why did you lie?"

"Because you two have your lives together and I don't, and all these years later I still wonder what it would be like to kiss you both, which is really annoying because he's being such a dick to me." Melody's rant concluded with a frustrated huff, as Dakota stood by in shock.

He didn't mind being called a dick, but the rest was quite a revelation. She still, after all these years, wondered what it would be like to kiss them…both of them.

Melody hadn't changed at all. This was all part of her game. Her life was a mess but she still had her looks. She'd probably just love to ride the high of having two guys after her again. Dakota was sure of it.

Well, if that's what she wanted, then that's what she'd get. He'd kiss her, all right. So would Justus, if Dakota had anything to say about it. They would call her bluff, only this time, unlike all those years ago, they would be united against her.

If she were playing games and saying she wanted them

both when all she really wanted was the attention of them fighting over her, she'd likely run out of the bar and never bother them again. But if she was serious, and was really willing to kiss them both, and more, then hell, he was up for giving her what she wanted.

No problem. What man didn't fantasize about having a threesome at least once in his life?

Damn, just the thought had his throat feeling tight—parts lower, as well.

"Melody." Dakota cleared his throat after his voice came out sounding a little hoarse.

"Yeah." She swung her gaze to him, looking pissed off, at what he wasn't sure. At him for being a dick? At herself for her rant, which didn't get a rise out of him?

"If you still want both Justus and me, like you say, then I'm up for it. But here's the thing—it's going to be with both of us, or nothing at all, and it's not going to end at just a kiss. We're men. We're not ten years old any more. The decision is yours." Dakota folded his arms. He glanced at Justus and saw he'd gone pale. "Right, bud?"

Justus stared wide-eyed at Dakota. He visibly swallowed and then opened his mouth but it took a few seconds for any sound to come out. "Uh, right."

He didn't sound all that sure of his answer, and he looked even more uncertain than he sounded, but Justus had said the word and that was good enough for Dakota.

Dakota turned back to Melody, surprised she was still here. "Well?"

She treated them to a crooked grin and shook her head. "You two don't have the balls to really do what you're suggesting."

"Oh, no?" Dakota's eyebrows shot up beneath the brim of his hat. No one said that to him and got away with it. "Try us."

"Fine. Let's go." Melody tipped her mug and downed the remains of her beer. She turned toward the door, and then glanced over her shoulder at them. "You coming or are you too afraid?"

Oh, they would be coming all right, in more ways than one, except for the fact Dakota was sure she'd turn tail and run the moment they called her bluff.

"Now, now. Don't be so impatient. Just finishing my beer, darlin'. Can't let good alcohol go to waste." Dakota glanced at Justus, clutching the mug like a lifeline. "Finish that and let's go."

"Are you sure about this?"

"Hell yeah, I'm sure. She's bluffing." Dakota kept his voice low and hid his mouth behind his big glass beer mug.

"You think?" Justus sent him a shocked look.

"Yup." In Dakota's experience, girls like Melody were big talkers and master manipulators, but when push came to shove, they were not doers.

"And what if she's not bluffing?"

Dakota didn't think that was an issue at all, but now that Justus mentioned it, his body was starting to wake up just at the idea. "Then we'll have a hell of a night to look back on when we're old and married."

Justus's eyes remained wide. Finally he glanced at Melody, standing by the door and looking impatient, and let out a long, slow breath. "Okay. Let's go."

Dakota grinned and downed the last sip of beer.

Beer mugs abandoned on the table, the two grabbed their jackets off the back of their chairs and headed for the door. As they got near, Melody cocked one brow. "So, where we going to do this? *If* we do this at all."

Dakota ignored her final dig. "Well, you're staying with family, so it'll have to be our place, I guess."

"At the Maverick's?" Justus's tone of voice had risen so high, it actually squeaked.

"Sure, why not? Blue's still away. Mrs. Jones is in the main house and she'll be asleep by now anyway. We've got the whole bunkhouse to ourselves."

"I don't know." Justus shook his head, still looking doubtful.

"Me either."

Dakota spun to Melody when she voiced her own doubt. He cocked a brow. "Oh really? Having second thoughts, are you?"

"The only thing I'm having second thoughts about is being in a vehicle with either of you driving after all the beer you drank. The Maverick place is far from here."

He frowned. "Not that far. And we had two beers each over the last two hours. We're both fine to drive. If you're that worried, then you can drive."

She was making excuses to get out of this, but Dakota wasn't going to let her off the hook that easily. As Justus watched speechless, which was probably for the better, Dakota dug the keys out of his jeans pocket.

He held them out to her. She eyed the keychain dangling before her for a second and then shook her head. "No, it's fine. If you really only had two, you can drive. That one beer I drank went to my head already anyway."

Ah-ha. So now she was pretending to be drunk from one beer. That way she could use that as an excuse later on. He knew all the tricks girls used and he wasn't going to let her play him, or Justus, ever again.

Dakota pulled the keys back into his palm. "Okay. I'll drive. Let's go."

"What about her car?" Justus asked as Dakota pushed open the front door and held it for Melody to walk through.

"We'll bring her back here to her car later." Not that Dakota thought they'd even get out of the parking lot before she backed out of this. He eyed her. "Okay?"

"Fine with me."

Wow, she was sticking it out longer than he thought she would. That was fine. He'd take care of this once and for all as soon as they were in the privacy of his truck. Once she was sandwiched between them in the front seat, she'd run away fast enough.

Dakota clicked open the locks on the truck. "Hop on up, darlin'."

With a backward glance at both of them, she reached for the handle to hoist herself inside. Dakota decided to help her, or perhaps unnerve her. Either way, he planted both palms on her nicely shaped butt cheeks and gave her a boost. She shot him a frown over her shoulder. He grinned back and rounded to the other side of the truck.

Once the three of them were seated, he in the driver's seat, Melody in the middle and Justus next to her, Dakota turned to them both. "So before we head to our place, I think we need to get one thing out of the way."

"What's that?" Justus glanced at him with the same expression of mixed misery and fear he'd worn since Dakota had suggested this in the bar.

"That kiss. Or rather kisses. They've been a long time coming. Melody's been waiting for this for twelve years. You first, Justus."

"Me?" His eyes flew wide again. He glanced from Dakota to Melody.

"Yup," Dakota said.

"You okay with that?" Justus glanced at Melody.

"Fine." Her voice held a bravado Dakota would bet his paycheck was fake, but she turned in her seat toward Justus.

Stubborn to the end. Dakota shook his head, begrudgingly impressed with her ability to hang in there through his every challenge so far. "Go on, Justus. Kiss her. I'm waiting for my turn next."

With a glance at Dakota, Justus drew in a visibly shaky breath and then leaned in toward Melody. While Dakota waited for her to call it off, their lips touched, then more than their lips as Justus cupped her face in his hands.

She didn't pull away, but then again, Justus had always been the less aggressive of the two of them. Dakota had always been more likely to take a girl home from the bar and try to screw her, while Justus was the type to ask a girl for her number and then take her out to dinner before he'd even kiss her. Justus had only ever slept with two girls in his life, and both of them he was dating seriously at the time.

It would have to be Dakota to force Melody's hand and scare her off, not Justus. He probably wasn't even using any tongue for this kiss. Dakota could remedy that, as soon as Justus finally finished up already.

As he watched, Justus angled his head and moved his hands into her hair. Maybe he was getting more into this than Dakota thought he would. That was fine. He could wait. Or hell, maybe he shouldn't wait. Wasn't that the point of a threesome—all three of them together?

Dakota leaned forward and slid his hands around her waist. She was tiny around the middle in comparison to her well-rounded hips and butt, not to mention her tits, which even though she had a jacket on the whole time, he had seen were nice.

He felt her breathing as her stomach rose and fell beneath his touch. He moved higher to cup the bottom of her breasts and felt her draw in a sharp breath.

Yup, he'd surprised her. Good. Time to up the game a bit more. As Justus continued to work her mouth, Dakota slid his right hand down, over the crotch in her jeans until he cupped her through the denim.

Waiting for her to slap his hand away, he began to rub. Only she didn't slap him. Hell, she kissed Justus harder as Dakota felt her breathing increase.

He moved his left hand up a bit and felt her nipple, hard and peaked beneath her shirt, and he began to get hard. He wrote it off as the normal reaction of a healthy male to having his hands on a female, even if she had acted like a bitch and a tease to him.

Justus finally pulled back, just when Dakota was beginning to doubt he ever would. She turned her head and glanced over her shoulder at Dakota. He slammed his lips into hers, spinning her body as he did. As Justus sat by, wide-eyed, Dakota pressed Melody back against the seat. He angled his mouth over hers and plunged his tongue between her lips.

As her beer-scented mouth opened to him, he began to stop hoping she'd back out of this. Kissing her felt so good

27

right now, he could only imagine how great the rest of her would feel.

In between fantasizing what he'd like to do to her, Dakota remembered Justus was still there. He pulled back from Melody's mouth.

Beneath the beams of the overhead parking lot light, he saw her eyes were heavily lidded when she looked at him. She was into this. He swallowed hard. He could definitely be into it if she was.

He glanced at Justus, who was breathing pretty heavily himself.

"You want us to let you out so you can get into your own car and go back to your grandparents?" He'd give her one last chance. After all, as much as he would like to have her right now, he wasn't the kind of man to take what wasn't offered.

Melody shook her head. "I don't want to get out."

There was still a niggling in the back of Dakota's mind. A lack of trust long ago instilled in him from this girl.

What if she did cry date rape? They didn't really know her anymore. She'd left when they were ten, and she'd been away from here for a long time.

They couldn't, at least they shouldn't, bring her back to the ranch and involve the Mavericks and their job in a possible mess.

He glanced at Justus. He'd agree to whatever Dakota decided. He knew that.

"Kiss Justus again." Dakota ran his hand between Melody and the seat and gave her a little nudge in Justus's direction.

Justus frowned at him. "I thought we were heading to the ranch."

Dakota shook his head. "Not yet. We're fine here for now." The lot wasn't lit too well. The truck was parked along the edge facing the woods. No one would see them in the dark interior. He glanced at Melody. "Go on, darlin'."

She leaned forward and Justus wasted no time meeting her lips. Then Dakota reached around and undid the button and zipper of her jeans.

Her stomach muscles jumped at his touch. He'd make more of her jump if she wanted and didn't stop him. He slid his hand down, inside her panties.

Feeling the smooth, hair-free skin nearly made Dakota groan. He loved when a woman was clean-shaven. Loved to bury his face between her thighs and tongue her to orgasm, but that wasn't going to happen here and now so instead, Dakota slipped a fingertip between her lower lips and located her most sensitive spot.

Justus pulled back from her lips and glanced down. He stared at where Dakota's hand disappeared inside Melody's pants, before he raised his gaze to her face. Her eyes were squeezed shut as she leaned her head against Dakota's chest.

He dipped one finger inside her, drawing out the dampness that proved she really did want them—or at least her body did. He wasn't sure what exactly was going on in her mind, but she sure wasn't running away from this. He went back to rubbing her. In response her hips tipped forward and she pressed harder against his finger.

He dragged his gaze away from the pleasure he saw on her face in the dim light of the truck, to look at Justus, motionless in front of them. "Justus."

His friend glanced up at him, looking kind of dazed. "Yeah?"

"Your turn." Dakota pulled his hand out of Melody's jeans.

Justus swallowed hard, but did as Dakota had told him to. He took his turn, turning his hand to press it against her belly, and then sliding it down, fingers first, into the front of her open jeans.

The angle would be more awkward for Justus but he'd have to deal with it, because Dakota was enjoying the feel of Melody leaning against him, panting from his touch. In fact, he had no intention of standing by and just watching the way Justus had. There was plenty he could do.

Dakota slid his hand beneath her shirt, then went one better and slipped beneath the smooth fabric of her bra to roll her nipple between his fingers. Her breath caught in her throat, making him smile.

He moved his mouth to her neck and, after brushing her hair to the side, latched on to the skin of her throat. She tilted her head, allowing him more access. He took advantage of it by drawing her earlobe between his lips.

Justus was breathing heavier, and working Melody so hard, he was rocking her body in time with his arm movements. It wouldn't be long now, judging by the tiny sounds of pleasure escaping her.

Images, ideas, began to career into Dakota's brain. He wanted her jeans off. He wanted to brace her naked body against his, hold her knees back and her thighs wide and watch Justus love her, with his fingers, his tongue, his dick, maybe all three, one at a time. As long as it was good and hard, and had Melody writhing, screaming, and begging for more as she pressed against him.

Dakota's dick almost throbbed just from the thought. He'd never been into watching, at least he'd never known he was, but the way he was feeling now…yeah, he wanted to watch Justus make love to her and then do it himself.

He wanted it bad.

She started to come, shaking, pushing back harder against Dakota and thrusting her hips forward at Justus. Dakota squeezed her nipple harder and held her more tightly against him with his other arm.

Melody cried and writhed under both of their scrutiny, until finally her cries slowed.

Justus eased up and stopped working her as both cowboys sat dazed. She turned and reached for both of their belt buckles at the same time, one with each hand.

Dakota was ready to burst. He'd love to open his jeans and push Melody's mouth down over him, then watch her do the same to Justus, but he didn't.

"I think we need to take this slow." Dakota was so horny, it was hard to believe he'd gotten those words to actually come out of his mouth.

Still breathing heavily, Melody laughed. "Slow?"

"Yeah, I know, things happened, and it sounds...strange, but that's what I think is best. You have some thinking to do."

"Thinking about what?"

"About if you're ready for this, with us, both of us."

"What did we just do? This was with both of you."

Dakota laughed. "This is nothing. Some touching. Some kissing. You know what I'm talking about. If we go any further...well, it's going to be a lot further. I don't need you suddenly deciding to be with one of us and dumping the other one. You need to make sure you want this, both of us. And if you wake up tomorrow morning and decide you're embarrassed about being with us both, and decide we forced you somehow... Well, I'm not going to pay the price because you have regrets. Neither is Justus."

"You still don't trust me, do you?" She stared up at him and he tried not to notice how swollen her lips looked from the kisses.

"Nope." Dakota shook his head.

"Not even after all this." A frown creased her brow.

"*Especially* not after all this."

Dakota's big brother was in the military now. He had a friend who was sitting in the brig because a girl had sex with him and then cried rape afterward when her boyfriend found out she'd cheated. Dakota may not be a college graduate, but he was smart enough to learn from other people's mistakes—especially if it kept him out of trouble.

He shouldn't have let things go this far. His only excuse was he honestly had thought she'd back out before they did anything at all. Well that, and he was horny as hell, so maybe his dick had been doing some of the thinking for a little while.

"You do realize, if I don't get this job, I'm gone again next week." Melody's statement hung in the air, taunting Dakota. Telling him it was dumb to waste time. It could be now or never with this girl.

He could just say what the hell and take her since there was a good chance they might never see her again after next week. If she got a job across the country, she might never come back to this little town.

"But what if you do get the job right here in our old school? Then what?" he asked.

She shrugged. "Then I'll move in with my grandparents and work until I get on my feet financially, then I'll get my own place."

Dakota shook his head. "Where you're going to live isn't what I'm worried about. If we go all the way with this, and then you get this job, I'm having trouble believing you'd be okay living in a town with both of us, knowing we all had sex together."

More importantly, would Dakota be able to see her—at the bar, walking down the street, sitting in a pew in church—and not get hard as a rock from the memories?

Doubtful. He'd never forget the sound of when Justus made her come, or the feel of her flesh beneath his fingers and her mouth beneath his.

"All right. I'll go home and consider everything on one condition. Whatever I decide, you two have to live with."

"Meaning what?" Dakota narrowed his eyes at her. "Because if you decide you want just me or just Justus, that's not going to happen. It's all or nothing. I told you that. He and I agreed no woman would ever get in the way of our friendship." And that decision had been thanks to the very woman seated between them now, not so coincidentally.

"That's right," Justus agreed.

Melody let out a huff of air. "I understand that. What I meant was if I call you tomorrow and tell you I want both of you, then that's what's going to happen. If I don't call it means I don't want either of you and you never contact me again. If we do run into each other, this, tonight, is never mentioned. You don't talk about it at all, ever. Not to me and definitely not to any of your buddies."

"Agreed." Dakota glanced at Justus.

He nodded. "I never kiss and tell, Melody, but yeah, agreed."

"And don't think I don't feel you, Dakota." Melody leaned back and pressed against his erection. "If I pushed the issue, you'd be doing anything I wanted tonight."

Dakota smiled. His hand was still under her shirt so he gave her nipple a squeeze. "Darlin', I'm a twenty-two-year-old healthy red-blooded male pressed against you. Of course, I'm hard. And make no mistake, I'm sure it would be very sweet to slide into you. Many times and into many places. But no, I wouldn't be doing whatever you wanted tonight, no matter what you say or do."

Justus swallowed audibly from the other side of Melody. His giving in to her, on the other hand, might be an issue. As virtuous as Justus tended to act with the girls he dated, Dakota knew one thing—this particular girl was Justus's kryptonite. His first love, or at least his first big crush that, to a fifth-grader, had felt like love.

All bets were off as far as Justus's usual behavior when Melody was concerned. One more reason Dakota was glad he was involved in this strange arrangement—to protect Justus from getting his heart ripped out and stomped on by this girl.

Whether intentional on her part, or forced because of her job situation, there was a good chance she'd be leaving this town and never looking back. Then Justus would be left, scarred, in her dust.

Maybe with Dakota making the third side of this messed-up triangle, Justus wouldn't get so attached. And if he did, at least he'd have someone to lean on when she left. He'd have Dakota and their friendship.

Leaning against his chest, Melody let out a sigh. He glanced down and saw Justus's hand was still in her jeans and beneath the sleeve of his jacket, Justus's forearm muscles were moving.

Dakota shook his head and smiled. "What are you doing to her?"

Justus glanced up. "Making sure she has enough

33

information to make her decision when she leaves here."

Information? It looked more like an impending orgasm to Dakota. Maybe Justus wasn't so virtuous after all. Melody drew in a sharp breath and Justus's eyes started to look out of focus.

Shit. Justus was well on his way to being in love with this girl again. Though that may have happened even without Dakota's failed plan to send Melody running, which instead had led to her coming. Twice.

They all, but Justus in particular, needed a reminder there were three of them here. This was not some romantic date. Dakota turned Melody's head to face him and kissed her, thrusting his tongue inside her mouth the way he'd like to thrust his cock into her.

Blindly he did something that was probably risky, considering he wasn't convinced she could be trusted yet, and pushed her jeans down her hips, just a few inches, giving Justus more room to work his fingers in and out of her.

It must have met with Melody's approval. She let out a shuddering breath.

Starting to hope, a little more than he liked, that she'd call them tomorrow and say she'd agree to this thing, Dakota slid his hand down Melody's back. Continuing down, he bumped into Justus's hand, already there.

Justus held still.

Dakota's gaze met his over Melody. "Together or not at all?"

"Together or not at all," Justus echoed.

Justus moved his forefinger inside Melody again, sliding against Dakota's finger, also inside her. Both of them stroked her. It was crazy. It was hot. But it wasn't enough to push her over the edge, though she felt close as her muscles gripped them both.

Dakota upped the game. He slid his finger, wet from her juices, back and began to circle the tight entrance of her ass. Melody's breath caught in her throat but she didn't pull away.

As Justus worked her outside with one hand while

stroking one finger inside her, Dakota pressed gently into her ass. Her body began to pulse around his fingertip as she started to shake.

"Oh God." Justus let out a shaky breath.

She came hard, her muscles convulsing rhythmically around Dakota's fingertip.

Imagining her gripping his length while she came with him inside her, Dakota was having trouble not ripping her damn jeans all the way off and plunging into her. Her cries were driving him crazy.

As she started to quiet, Dakota discovered he'd latched onto her neck and sucked hard enough to mark her without his even realizing he'd done it. He cringed when even in the semi-darkness he could see he'd left a bruise.

Justus pulled back, still looking dazed as she trembled between them.

Her breath came in gasps as she glanced back at Dakota. "I thought you said no more tonight?"

"This doesn't count. It was just an extension of what we'd already done." Dakota cocked one brow. "Besides, our pants are still on, aren't they?"

"Yes, they certainly are. I didn't touch either of you at all." With a smirk, she zipped her jeans and pulled down her shirt. "So I guess you'll both have fun jerking off tonight."

Melody sat forward, looking as if she was about to leave them.

"Wait, don't forget to take our numbers before you go." Panic in his voice, Justus flipped the visor down and slid out the pen Dakota kept there. He scribbled what looked like both of their cell phone numbers on a napkin that had been stuck in the side-door compartment.

"Pretty confident I'll call, are you?" She took the napkin from Justus.

Dakota shrugged. "Call. Don't. Whatever. That's up to you." He opened the door and slid to the ground so she could climb out after him.

Once on the ground, Melody glanced from Justus to

Dakota. "Good night, you two."

From the passenger seat, Justus leaned toward the open door. "Good night."

"'Night." Dakota tipped his ball cap and climbed back in to the truck.

He found Justus staring at him like he was crazy. "What the hell do you mean, call, don't, whatever?"

Dakota glanced at Justus before starting the ignition. "Relax. She's going to call."

Justus stared across the parking lot to where Melody was climbing into her car. "She'd better."

"She will." Dakota waited for Melody to start the car and pull out of the parking lot before he did the same, turning onto the highway toward the ranch, the opposite direction of where she'd turned toward her grandparents' house.

One thing she'd said Dakota was certain would prove true. Both he and Justus would each be privately jerking off tonight. Maybe more than once.

CHAPTER THREE

Melody sat across from Mrs. Stowe, her old fifth-grade teacher, in what had to be the most surreal moment of her life.

Actually, now that she thought about it, last night with Dakota and Justus took the prize for most surreal life moments.

The fact that she had their phone numbers scrawled on a napkin in her purse and she was seriously considering calling them topped it all.

She tried to focus on her current surroundings, rather than memories of what had happened inside Dakota's truck. This interview was too important to blow.

The plaque on the desk inside the dull, beige-colored office read *Elizabeth Stowe, Assistant Principal.*

Melody had never considered that Mrs. Stowe had a first name. Of course she would, everybody did, but it's not something a fifth-grader thought about.

Their teacher was always just Mrs. Stowe to them. The woman who'd broken up the fight that Dakota seemed still obsessed with even today.

That their teacher had punished the two boys for that fight

might have something to do with his residual anger, but still, a twelve-year-old grudge seemed excessive.

And he was definitely holding a grudge. Melody had no doubt he'd jerked her around last night as payback. Making outrageous rules about her having to take both him and Justus, or neither one. Suggesting they go to the Maverick ranch together, and then backing out and saying nothing was going to happen last night no matter what. Then a couple of amazing orgasms later, a flippant renewal of the offer of the threesome.

There had been multiple orgasms for her and zero for them, and that was the most confusing of all. They hadn't let her touch them, not even when she tried to open their belts.

She'd thought Dakota had been bluffing right from the beginning while they were still inside the bar, saying they'd both be with her at once. That was the only reason she'd agreed to get into the truck with them in the first place. She definitely didn't think Justus would be up for it, even if Dakota was.

Justus had always been the quieter of the two. Maybe that's why she found them both so intriguing. They were so different in some ways, but so alike in others.

Once her zipper was down though, neither one had any issue sharing, and she had no problem coming.

Maybe they shared women all the time. It's not like she really knew them anymore. Twelve years was a long time to be away.

The whole thing was crazy. They'd barely touched her and she'd been throbbing with need. A need that hadn't subsided in the hours since she'd left them.

And now, when she should be listening to Mrs. Stowe talk about the job she needed so desperately, she couldn't focus on anything but the two cowboys. Melody was certainly aware of the twisting low in her belly, and her need to be filled by those boys. But how could she do what they were asking?

Then again, how could she have done what they'd done

last night?

She knew the answer to that. Her life was a shambles. Student loans. No job. Her parents were tired of her living with them and not working. She had no boyfriend. No sex. Then the two guys she'd had a crush on since she was ten walk into her life again after twelve years. They gave her orgasms and a promise of many more. But it all came wrapped in the craziest offer she'd ever heard.

Both or nothing.

Last night she'd come harder than ever before. Maybe their offer of both wasn't so insane after all.

"...includes the standard benefits package, including health and dental insurance."

Health insurance and dental. God, she really needed this job. She couldn't stay on her parents' insurance now that she was no longer a full-time student.

Melody nodded and pretended she'd heard all of what Mrs. Stowe had said, not just the tail end of it. "That sounds wonderful. I'm definitely extremely interested in the position."

"Good. It would be nice to have a former student in the ranks as teacher."

Her heart began to race. Did she have the job?

"Now, as I said, we interviewed another candidate before you. She has a slight edge over you since she does have teaching experience."

Which Melody did not.

Her heart sank. Oh well, back to her parents' house. Maybe she could get a job at the Supermart. Melody heard they offered benefits after six months of employment.

Fighting tears, she raised her gaze to Mrs. Stowe. "Of course, I understand. Thank you for taking the time to speak to me."

Mrs. Stowe held up one hand. "It's not finalized yet, Melody. There are more people than just me involved in making the decision, but you can be sure, I'll put in a good word for you and I'll call you the moment we make a decision, either way."

"Thank you. I appreciate that." Melody forced a smile.

Mrs. Stowe, who'd seemed so old and so scary to her at ten, was on her side. She was not only a perfectly normal person, she was a nice one too.

Her former teacher smiled. "You're very welcome. So now that the business is all settled, tell me, what have you been doing since you've been back? Is it strange after all these years?"

She stifled a laugh. Strange was a good word for it. "Well, I only got here yesterday but I did run into a few people I knew from the old days. Do you remember Dakota Washburn and Justus White from my class?"

"Oh goodness, of course I remember them. Really nice boys. Do you know what they did last year?"

Melody shook her head no. After last night, she couldn't even imagine what those two might have done, but it seemed Mrs. Stowe was happy about it so it couldn't be too bad.

"We have a student who's wheelchair-bound, but she's always had a love for horses. Those two boys—" Mrs. Stowe's voice cracked and she swiped at her eyes—"I'm sorry. I have trouble talking about it. It was so sweet. When they heard about her, those two designed and made a special saddle and took her riding on the Maverick property. It was absolutely amazing. She never looked so happy. Her parents either."

"Wow. That's amazing." As the older woman got so choked up she had to reach for a tissue and blot her eyes, Melody tried to reconcile the two cowboys who would do something so wonderful for a handicapped child, with the two men who'd had their hands down her pants last night. It was a difficult task.

"Amazing boys...young men, now. I'm proud to say they were two of mine." Mrs. Stowe sent her a tearful smile.

"Yes, that does sound...amazing," Melody agreed.

Maybe their former teacher, who still lived and worked in town, knew Dakota and Justus better than Melody did at this point. Her sincerity certainly was convincing.

Maybe this threesome thing was as out of character for them as it was for Melody. She'd never done, or even dreamed of doing, anything like last night, yet she had been right there between them in the truck. She'd felt both of their fingers inside her at the same time, and instead of feeling shame, or even fear, all she'd felt was pleasure. All she'd wanted was more.

She wanted this job too, but with someone with experience up against her for it, chances were good she wouldn't get it even with Mrs. Stowe's recommendation.

"Anyway. I've kept you long enough." Mrs. Stowe stood. "I'll be in touch as soon as I know something."

Melody stood as well, as relieved this interview was over as she was anxious about getting the position. She extended her hand, finding it strange she now was a half a head taller than her former teacher. "Thank you for taking the time to meet with me."

"My pleasure, Melody. And say hello to those two boys for me if you happen to see them again."

Fearing all of her mixed up feelings about seeing Dakota and Justus again were written all over her face, she just nodded. After a quick goodbye to Mrs. Stowe, Melody headed out of the office as fast as she could.

Sparing only a second for a shocked glance at the water fountain, which she realized was so low she'd have to kneel to use it, she made her way out the front exit doors and toward the visitor parking.

Outside, Melody sat in the driver's seat of her car and stared at the two phone numbers scrawled on the creased paper napkin. Justus's handwriting didn't look like it had changed all that much from fifth grade when he'd given her that Valentine's Day card.

He'd given her both of their numbers. They really were close friends, living, working, drinking together.

Time to find out what else they did together—besides her last night.

She took a deep breath and dialed the top number on the napkin. A masculine voice answered. She hesitated a beat. It was hard to tell which one it was over the phone. "Hi, it's Melody."

"Melody. Hi, it's Justus."

Justus had written his number first. That made sense and made it easier. Justus was less intimidating than Dakota. Even so, she longed to stall, delay the conversation that had her hands shaking and her heart pounding. "Are you busy?"

"Nah. Not so much. Just finished throwing some hay to the horses. Now I'm gonna go find Dakota. He was out checking on the herd. What are you doing?"

"I'm at school." She let out a short laugh at how strange that sounded. "I just had my interview today."

"Great. How'd it go?"

"All right, but there's someone else they interviewed too so I don't know what'll happen. I have to wait for them to decide."

"I'm sure you'll get it." Justus's firm tone left no doubt in her mind that he wanted her to stick around town.

"Thanks."

His confidence in her was nice. She only wished she shared it. And she had to wonder if Dakota felt the same.

Dakota was by far the bigger puzzle to her. Angry about some imagined twelve-year-old transgression on her part one moment, cradling her against his chest as she came the next. Marking her neck, as if he was staking his claim on her.

She reached up and touched the spot where she'd covered the bruise with makeup for her interview. Good thing it was cold out so she could wrap a scarf around her neck too.

"So, uh, did you think at all about this thing with us?" Justus's voice brought her back from memories of last night and to the present, as well as the situation she had yet to deal with. He was so damn cute as he asked the question. Kind of hesitant and hopeful at the same time. Melody smiled even as her pulse pounded harder.

"I've thought a lot about it." She'd done nothing but think

about it.

Justus paused a beat. "And?"

"And I have a question for you first."

"For me? Okay. Shoot."

Melody swallowed and forged ahead. "Have you and Dakota ever done this kind of thing before? Both of you with one girl?"

"No. Never." There was no hesitation before his answer.

She believed him. "Then why now? Why me?"

"Twelve years ago Dakota and I made a pact we'd never let a girl break up our friendship. If one of us went after you, the other one would be left out in the cold. This is the only way."

"Sharing me is the only way to preserve your friendship?" she asked with a laugh.

"I know it sounds nuts. Hell, it is kind of crazy, but I think it's working. At least I thought last night was pretty great. Wasn't it?"

"Yeah, it was." She couldn't lie to him about it. She sure as hell couldn't pretend she hadn't come. It had been pretty obvious to everyone in that truck, and probably anyone walking by who might have heard her. Melody's cheeks flushed with heat at that thought. "Justus, what if I get the job? You know then I'll be moving back to town again."

"That'd be great." His enthusiasm traversed the phone lines.

Great wasn't the adjective that came to Melody's mind.

If they had their little threesome, their relationship afterward would be awkward. Embarrassing. Doomed. All better descriptors than great, but only if she let this situation go any further than it already had. She could write off last night as a bad decision. Some heavy petting that didn't go too far.

Hell, last night wasn't much more than kissing really.

She remembered Justus and Dakota's hands on her, inside her, Dakota touching her in a place no one ever had before.

Her justification was bullshit. It had been much more than

43

kissing and the mere memory of it had her insides twisting, wanting more.

Melody drew in a shaky breath. "All right."

"All right? You mean—"

"I made my decision and yes, I think I want to see you two again."

Justus whooped in her ear. "That's great. Wait until I tell Dakota."

Great, now he'd go rushing off and tell Dakota they were going to get lucky tonight. She began to feel like this was a huge mistake. More, she began to feel like a whore. "Justus?"

"Yeah?"

"I'm not sure I'm ready for sex yet."

"Wait. You're a virgin?" The shock in his tone made her laugh.

"No. I don't sleep around but no, I'm not a virgin. I've definitely had sex before." Though her college boyfriend never knew how to touch her the way these two cowboys had last night.

"Phew. Okay. How about this…what if we meet and have a beer and see how the three of us get along?"

"Like a three-way date?"

"Yes, but only we'll know that. To everyone else, it'll look like three old friends hanging out."

"And then?"

"And then it'll end just like any other date. Dakota and I will try and kiss you goodnight and hope you'll let me . . . I mean us."

She smiled. "I'll let you kiss me."

"And more?" There was a smile in Justus's voice.

If last night was any indication, yeah, she'd let him do more. Melody laughed. "Maybe. Okay, we'll give this thing a try. Tonight?"

"We've got some stuff happening here at the ranch that needs our attention. One of the heifers is close to calving. Can I get back to you after I check with Dakota?"

Calving. Jeez, she'd forgotten how rural her hometown

was after living in the city for so long. "Sure. Just let me know."

"Will do, and Melody, I had a really good time last night and I'm really looking forward to our date, and that kiss."

She smiled. What the hell, might as well tell him the truth. "Me too, Justus."

Damn.

Now her panties were wet, just from his voice and the promise of a kiss. She was in big trouble.

If she was put under the spell of those two again, she had a feeling there'd be a whole lot more than a good night kiss . . . and maybe that wouldn't be so bad.

Hell, chances were she wouldn't get this job. Having two guys to soothe her damaged psyche and make her forget reality for a little bit might be exactly what she needed. Two really nice guys, at that, in spite of their crazy plan.

Between student loans, her parents and rejections from countless job applications, it was amazing to Melody she managed to get up and dressed every day. Some mornings she had to fight the urge to crawl into a ball and hide under the covers all day.

The only reason she'd even been in the bar last night was because she'd seen a help-wanted sign in the window and figured it couldn't hurt to explore her options. Fine arts degree or not, a job was a job, even if it was slinging beer at the local hangout. Unfortunately, it had been for a part-time dishwasher and paid minimum wage, no tips.

Wrong or not, being with Justus and Dakota made her feel alive again. Made her forget her worries, at least for a little while. Made her remember the good old days and simpler times, when the only thing to worry about was if the boy in the row next to her liked her or not.

She smiled. He liked her all right. So did the boy next to him. And she liked them too.

CHAPTER FOUR

"Oh my God." The horse glanced up as Justus flipped his cell phone shut and said the words aloud, even though he was alone except for the animals.

Melody wanted to see them again. Maybe they'd be together tonight.

He had to find Dakota.

Justus ran out of the barn, stopping only long enough to close and secure the door. He flipped the latch shut, spun around and nearly crashed head on into Dakota.

The blood was rushing so loudly in his ears he hadn't even heard the sound of Dakota's boots on the packed snow and gravel behind him.

Red-cheeked, Dakota stuffed his hands into his coat pockets. "One of the younger heifers is about to have her calf. Her water sac's just starting to show and she's acting like she's having contractions."

Ignoring that Dakota had once again forgotten his gloves, Justus shook his head at this new information. "Shit. That calf's definitely coming tonight. Where's the heifer now?"

Dakota hooked a thumb toward the dog at his heels. "Misty and I got her into the calving shed while she was still on her feet. I didn't want her lying down out there in the field. It's going to be a long cold night for all of us and I, for one, want to at least be out of the wind for it."

Tail wagging and ears forward, Misty circled Dakota's legs. She got excited when there was work to be done. Herding dogs as a breed enjoyed their jobs, but Justus would likely lock her in the bunkhouse for the night. That heifer didn't need to be worrying about where the dog was while she was giving birth. Too many things could go wrong.

Then again, it could go perfectly smoothly. Either way, they didn't need Misty as a distraction during it.

Justus shook his head. "Blue was hoping to be home before any of them calved."

"Well then he should have moved his trip up by a week because unless he's at the airport right now, he's going to miss this one." Dakota cocked a brow.

"I know he was worried about this heifer in particular because it's her first time." They'd have to call Blue and let him know what was going on.

Dakota blew out a long breath. "Hell, I'm worried about her too. Besides being a first-calf heifer, she's small. We should have kept her away from the big bulls and only let her breed with one on the small side.

Justus frowned. "None of the Maverick bulls are small. We're known for the size of our animals."

Dakota sighed. "Doesn't matter now. We gotta deal with it ourselves."

"Damn, I hope that calf is at least facing the right way." Justus glanced up at Dakota. "What if it's not?"

His friend shrugged beneath the bulk of his jacket. "Then we'll have to call the vet."

Emergency vet visits cost money. That cut into profits. "Blue rotated that one calf himself last year."

"That one wasn't breech, it was just turned the wrong way. And besides, Blue's not here."

No, he wasn't, but Justus sure wished he were. This would be the first time Blue wasn't here during calving season. That meant this would be the first time he and Dakota were all on their own. They definitely had to call Blue.

Justus realized his cell phone was still in his hand and the reason he'd come to find Dakota in the first place hit him. "Aw, crap."

"What?"

"Melody called." Justus held the phone up. "That's what I was on my way to tell you. She wants to go out."

"She wants to go out?" Dakota's eyebrows shot up. "With both of us, like I said? Why did she call your phone? What exactly did she say?"

Fragments from the conversation swirled in Justus's mind, along with the realization Dakota was acting a little jealous that Melody had called his phone.

He'd gone along with this crazy plan because everything had moved so fast, and was so crazy with them and Melody in the truck. Her pants half off, his hands all over her, but now Justus realized this situation was a firestorm waiting to happen. It had to be completely even between them both or nothing at all.

If Justus went out with Melody alone, it could very well cost him his friendship with Dakota. At the very least it would change it. He'd known it on some level before but now he really felt it as Dakota glared at him—Melody had to be with them both or not at all.

And how the hell would that work in the long run? Justus couldn't imagine it. He couldn't think that far ahead.

It hurt his head and his heart because he knew the answer. The three of them couldn't work for more than a short fling. The local pastor wouldn't exactly agree to marry them all, now would he?

Justus shook the disturbing thoughts from his head. He couldn't deal with them now. And maybe that was the answer. Have fun and enjoy being with her while they could and deal with the future later.

He blew out a breath and watched it freeze in the air before him. "She said lots of things, and she called my phone because I wrote my number first, but I guess we'll have plenty of time to talk about it while we're waiting it out in the calving shed all night."

This would take all night, too. Older cows could deliver in two hours, but first-calf heifers could take six hours, and that's even if things went smoothly.

He better go tell Mrs. Jones they wouldn't be eating dinner inside either. They'd have to eat something they could bring with them to the shed.

Damn, this night was gonna suck. Just when he thought they'd be enjoying a beer, and hopefully more, in the company of Melody, they'd have to put off their fun until tomorrow night.

Justus looked up at Dakota, who was frowning at him. "Okay, listen. I'm gonna go tell Mrs. Jones what's going on and that we'll be missing dinner. You go back to the shed, check on the heifer and call Blue. Then I'll meet you there and we'll call Melody together and figure out when we'll be able to see her. All right?"

"All right, but you and I are going to talk about that phone call and how this is going to work." Dakota scowled.

"We will. No problem." Justus went to turn toward the house and then turned back. "Dakota?"

He glanced over his shoulder, Misty at his heels. "Yeah?"

"Together or not at all."

Dakota nodded and headed for the calving shed.

"Oh, and lock the dog up in the bunkhouse for the night," Justus called after him.

"Will do." Dakota raised a bare hand but didn't stop.

"And get your damn gloves while you're there!" Justus yelled.

He heard Dakota laugh. "Yes, Mom."

CHAPTER FIVE

"It's the young first-calf heifer you were worried about." In the calving shed, Dakota stood near the door and held the phone to his ear as he told his boss what was happening. Signal really sucked out in the pasture, even in the big old main house, but luckily they got some spotty signal in the barn and here in the calving shed, if you stood by the door in just the right spot.

"Shit. I wanted to be there for that one. My flight's not scheduled for until tomorrow. Maybe I can try and get on one today." The frustration was clear in Blue's tone.

"Blue, by the time you get here, she'll be done."

"Being her first time, it's gonna take her a good six hours—"

"And even if you can get a reservation on a flight today, by the time you get to the airport, sit on a plane from New York to Denver, connect to Yampa Valley, and then drive to the ranch, it'll all be over."

Blue sighed. "I know, you're right. You call the vet if anything at all goes even a little bit wrong. Don't try to handle it yourself. Promise me."

"I will, Blue." Dakota glanced at the heifer.

Her water sac was already starting to protrude and if he looked closely, he could just see a hoof showing. As long as that was a front foot and not a rear one, it wasn't breech and they were good . . . if the calf's head was pointing down and not bent backward. And if the calf was upright and not lying on his back inside his mother.

There were a lot of *ifs* to watch for.

"Call me if anything happens—good or bad."

Dakota glanced at the combination clock/thermometer hanging on the wall and cringed. It was already nearly suppertime. "It could be pretty late. I don't wanna wake you up."

"I don't care. Do it anyway." Blue's tone was firm, leaving no doubt in Dakota's mind he had better call his boss or pay the price later.

"All right. I'll call no matter what."

"And make sure the calf's breathing when it comes out and if it's not—"

"I'll clear the mucous and give it a slap and if that doesn't work I'll get the hose and breath into its nose." Dakota shook his head.

You'd think it was Blue's baby being born and not one of the hundred-plus calves they'd see come into the world this season alone.

"Just one nostril—"

"While I hold the other nostril and its mouth closed. I know, Blue. I've seen you do it hundreds of times."

"Okay, I'll talk to you later then."

"Yes, sir."

"Bye, Dakota." There was a sigh in Blue's voice.

"Bye, Blue." Dakota smiled and disconnected the call just as Justus came through the door.

"Look what Mrs. Jones did for us when I told her we wouldn't be able to leave here to eat dinner in the main house." He held up a basket holding two short fat thermoses and two tall thin ones.

Dakota frowned. "What's in 'em?"

"Hot beef stew and even hotter coffee." Justus grinned and put the basket holding the containers, napkins, and cutlery down on the bench along the wall.

"Good." They were going to need both the food and the coffee for the long night they had ahead.

"You call Blue?" Justus glanced at Dakota then back to the heifer.

"Yup, just hung up with him." Dakota blew on his cold hands. "He's being a worrier."

"Nothing more than I expected. He's not used to being away." Justus scowled a little when he saw Dakota had obviously forgotten his gloves again, but at least he didn't lecture him on it.

"Yeah. You call Melody back yet?" Dakota crossed his arms and shoved his bare hands under the armpits of his coat.

Justus's brows knit in a frown beneath the brim of his hat. "No, I told you I was waiting so we could call together."

"It doesn't matter anyway." Dakota shrugged. "We don't have anything good to tell her. Tonight's a bust, and tomorrow night Blue's back."

"Crap. I forgot he gets back tomorrow." Justus let out a huff. "We can still go out with her."

"But we can't bring her back here." If anything did happen, it would have to be in the truck again. Not that he'd be picky about the place, but a man needed room to work.

"What about here, tonight?" Justus looked up at Dakota.

"Here?"

"Sure. It's not so bad. And you know most of tonight will be sitting around and waiting on this calf. If everything goes smooth, we won't have hardly anything to do."

"No, but I'm not sure how Melody's going to feel about this." Dakota glanced around the calving shed.

Yeah, it was clean and not freezing cold, but not exactly toasty warm either. He supposed they could turn up the electric heater and throw a blanket over some of the hay bales.

"We won't know until we ask." Justus grinned. "Besides, I'm thinking she's been living in the city long enough that this kinda thing would impress her. Miss Casey sure seemed to take to the ranch stuff."

Dakota laughed. "It was Blue that Miss Casey took to, more than the ranch, and you know it."

"Yeah, that's true. He still thinks we don't know that he spends most of the night in her room and sneaks out just before dawn." Justus smirked. "Anyway, I'm calling Melody. You on board with inviting her here?"

The heifer let out a groan of discomfort and kicked out with her rear hoof. Another contraction, but they were still coming far apart. At that point they had nothing to lose. This was going to take a while.

Dakota let out a breath. "Sure, what the hell."

With one final glance and a nod toward Dakota, Justus pulled out his phone and moved nearer to the doorway. He pushed a few buttons as Dakota realized his heart had kicked into high gear.

Then Justus was speaking. "Hey, Mel. It's Justus. There's been a slight change of plans but I was, well we both were, kind of hoping you'd be up for it. " Justus listened for a second and then glanced at Dakota. The anticipation was making it nearly impossible for him to stand still. "I'll let Dakota tell you what's happening."

Dakota found the phone thrust at him. Clearing his throat, he took a step forward and grabbed it from Justus. "Hey. It's Dakota."

"Hi." Melody's soft voice filled his ear, even as he grew hard.

Dakota dragged in a breath. "We thought you might like to get a taste of life on the Maverick ranch."

"Um, sure. If that's all right."

"Sure, it's all right. We're the only ones here right now so we can't leave, and we've got a heifer about to calve. Now likely everything will go smooth—" he hoped, "—but we still have to be here waiting on her. We thought maybe you'd like

53

to join us. I know it's not exactly a date but . . ."

"No, it's fine. I'm not really in the mood for hanging out at the bar tonight anyway."

"Good. So you know how to get here?"

"Everybody knows where the Maverick place is," she laughed. "But that's about it. I mean I know where the main gate is, but I can't say I'd know where to go after that."

Dakota smiled. "No problem. Cell phone signal is spotty here so you might not be able to call us when you arrive, but if you give me an idea of when you'll be here, Justus or I will drive out and meet you in the drive at the front gate."

"Okay. I guess half an hour?"

Dakota glanced at the clock on the wall and smiled. "See you in half an hour then. Oh, and Mel, dress warm. We're in the calving shed so we're kinda roughin' it tonight."

He could imagine that one of her eyebrows had shot up at that, like it had at the bar when they'd been talking and she hadn't liked something he'd said. Damn, he found that move sexy, even when she was on the phone and it was all in his imagination.

"Uh, all right. I'll put on a heavier sweater."

And how he would love to take off that heavy sweater. Dakota reined in his thoughts. *One step at a time.* "Good. We'll see you soon."

"Okay, bye."

Dakota disconnected the call and handed the phone back to Justus, who'd stood by and waited surprisingly patiently throughout the entire conversation.

"She's coming?" Justus asked.

"She's coming." Dakota was happy she was coming, but he'd be happier when she was *coming.* Memories of last night in the truck flew through his brain.

"Now what?" A look of doubt darkened Justus's features.

Justus didn't seem to be taking to this situation as easily as he was. Dakota shot him a glance and then looked back to the heifer. "I guess we'll see."

"Dakota, I've never done anything like this before."

"Neither have I. You know that." Though he'd thought about it a good hundred times in the past twenty-four hours alone.

"Exactly how's it gonna work? I mean, I know how it went in the truck, but that was just, you know . . . but if we . . ." It seems the thought of both of them having sex with Melody at the same time had rendered Justus incapable of putting a full sentence together.

Not surprising.

Dakota shook his head. "It'll be fine."

"I hope so." Justus blew out a shaky breath. "Besides, there's no guarantee anything at all is going to happen. In fact, I guarantee it won't, which is good really. We should get to know her again before—"

Dakota frowned. "You *guarantee it won't?* Why?"

Justus raised his gaze to Dakota and cringed. "Oh yeah, I never got around to telling you. During the first phone call, Melody told me she didn't think she was ready to have sex yet."

"She actually said those words? That she's not ready to have sex?" Dakota's frown deepened. She'd seemed plenty ready last night in the truck.

"Yup. I asked her and she's not a virgin or anything, so don't worry. She's just not ready."

"You came right out and asked if she was a virgin?" Dakota nearly choked.

One day he'd have to teach Justus how to talk to women.

It figured it was his phone she'd called. Just Dakota's luck. He'd better take over communications. With Justus in charge they'd all be back to exchanging paper valentines in cardboard mailboxes and nothing more, like they were in fifth grade again.

"She took me by surprise, okay. I was throwing hay to the horses and suddenly she's on the phone saying she wants to meet us." Justus scowled. "Anyway, we agreed to a normal date, well at least a date with the three of us, not so normal but whatever. I said we'd just see how things go."

"Okay." Dakota sighed. What was done, was done. He'd just have to deal with it. He glanced around the calving shed. "I'm not sure this exactly counts as a date though."

"Well, we have stew and coffee, and I think there's buttered rolls in the bag. That's kind of like taking her out for dinner."

Dakota laughed. "Kind of, but not quite."

"Hey, we're cowboys. This is us. She better get used to us. If she doesn't like the way things are, then maybe she's not the girl we should be hanging around with."

That was the first smart thing Dakota had heard Justus say during this conversation. Dakota shot him a look and a nod. "You're right. I agree one hundred percent."

If they were just in it to screw a girl, she could be anyone, and who cared what she thought of them or their lives. But this was Melody, the girl Justus had built up to goddess-like perfection over the past twelve years, and it did matter what she thought of them, and their way of life.

It would definitely be interesting, if nothing else. But Dakota didn't hold much hope there'd be anything more than calving going on here tonight.

That was fine. He doubted Justus was ready to handle it all yet anyway. However, Dakota was.

His dick, hard as a rock just from the conversation, was ready for more. It would sure be nice to have Melody's soft hands, or even better her hot mouth, wrapped around it.

Damn, now he was uncomfortably hard. It was going to be a long night.

CHAPTER SIX

Dakota stood behind the heifer and did things to her Melody thought only a veterinarian should be doing. It involved lubricant, gloves and a very large and distended business end of the cow.

She gave an involuntary shiver, more from the thought of that calf coming out of its mother, than from the cold in the building.

"That calf looks pretty big." All she could see so far was two hooves, but they weren't small.

"It'll probably be about eighty pounds," Justus said as he stood next to her watching Dakota as well.

"Jeez."

Justus smiled. "She can handle it. Don't worry." He kept his eyes trained on Dakota. "As long as it's facing the right way. That's what Dakota's checking now."

Melody watched exactly how Dakota was checking, with his hands, both of them, inside the heifer. But he'd been standing there for what seemed like a long time, his hands in the cow but not moving. "Why's it taking so long? Can't he figure out if those are front hooves or back hooves?"

"Well you can't just go sticking your arms deep inside her

57

and feel around, especially not during labor. You have to dilate the, uh, opening. That's what takes all the time, and the patience. Then he's going to making sure the head is facing down and that its neck isn't bent back. If it's not in position, we're supposed to call the vet."

While Justus told her all the specific details about calving, Melody swallowed hard as very naughty thoughts careened into her head. Seeing Dakota in doctor mode, and having Justus describing things softy near her ear as they both kept their voices down during this delicate procedure, had her insides twisting.

"Is it what you expected?" Justus glanced at her.

"Not one little bit." She never in all her twenty-two years would have thought that watching a calf being born, and all the less than pleasant stuff that entailed, would turn her on.

It was kind of sick. When she'd first arrived after following Justus's truck with her car from the gate, Dakota had been washing the cow's rear with warm water. To clean away any bacteria, Justus had told her, before Dakota moved on to the next step—the internal examination to feel if the calf was in the correct position.

Watching him now, she couldn't help but remember his fingers pressed inside her. Crazy. She needed help. This had nothing to do with last night. Yet it did.

He was as gentle handling the heifer as he'd been handling her. That was important in a man. More important in a lover. Or in two lovers.

She glanced at Justus quickly and tried to calm her rapid heart rate.

"I'm gonna see if he needs help." Justus moved to where Dakota stood, both hands deeply inside the heifer now. "How's it feel?"

"I haven't gone as deep as the calf's head yet. I'm still making sure she's dilated enough so I don't hurt her." Dakota glanced at the clock, and then at Justus. "How long has it been?"

Justus followed his gaze to look at the clock on the wall.

"I'd say just about five minutes. That should be enough. Right?"

"Yeah." Dakota braced his feet wide on the floor, knees slightly bent, and pushed farther inside the cow. He'd tied her tail to the side but it twitched now as she stomped one foot. "I wanna get out of here before the next contraction."

"Good idea." Justus laughed.

Dakota concentrated on his task as Melody watched, riveted. She'd never underestimate ranchers again. They had a lot of responsibilities with these animals, including acting as midwives it seemed.

"It's facing down headfirst and it's upright. That's good. And the head," he shifted a bit, "is facing down." Dakota let out a breath and slowly pulled his hands out. He glanced at Justus. "No vet. We should be good."

Justus let out a breath. "Good. I better call Blue so he doesn't worry." Justus moved toward the doorway and took out his phone.

"Yeah, good idea." Free and clear now, Dakota peeled off his plastic gloves and tossed them in the nearby trashcan, then untied the cow's tail. She swatted it back and forth, showing her opinion pretty clearly about having had it tied to the rail with that rope for so long.

Dakota washed his hands in the sink along the far wall and then came back to stand by Melody. "Hey. Sorry I didn't have time to say a proper hello when you arrived. I had to check her between contractions. It couldn't wait."

He leaned down and planted a kiss directly on her lips. It was quick and light, but it had her barely able to answer.

"It's okay. You have work to do. Don't let me get in your way." She hoped her cheeks didn't look as flushed as they felt.

Dakota studied her closely and then smiled. "What's up with you tonight?"

"What? Nothing. Why would you ask?" She stuttered.

Shit, he could read her too well. He somehow knew she was turned on. So much so that if he pulled off her pants

59

right now, she'd spread her legs and beg for it.

"You're acting kind of strange. And your voice is a little too high." His eyes opened wide. He grinned broader and took a step closer. He ran his hand down her arm. "You're horny."

"What? No. Girls don't get horny."

"Bullshit." He frowned. "So if I slid my hand inside those little panties of yours, I wouldn't find you wet?"

"Dakota!" She tried to act indignant but she knew it was true. And she didn't put it past him to check. Hell, she kind of hoped he did. "Okay. Maybe. A little."

Justus had wrapped up his phone call and was back, but stood by looking a little confused at finding Dakota bent so low that he was practically cheek-to-cheek with her. So close she could smell the soap he'd used to wash his hands.

"Justus, our little city girl here is turned on by calving." At Dakota's words, warm air wisped across the skin of her cheek.

"I didn't say that."

"You didn't have to." Dakota turned his head just enough to glance at Justus. "Come over here."

Brow raised, Justus did as instructed.

Dakota continued. "We've got some time before this calf comes."

"Yup." Justus narrowed his eyes. "What did you have in mind?"

"I think maybe Melody needs to relax a bit. She seems strung a little tight tonight." Dakota slapped her butt and sent her jumping with a squeal, which only proved his point.

"Melody?" Justus's gaze focused on her.

There was no denying it. Her panties were wet, her body was strung tight as a bow, and the solution to both problems were the two cowboys in front of her.

To hell with worrying—about her job, her parents, her student loans, her virtue. To hell with it all. She glanced behind her. There was a stack of hay bales about waist-high covered with a horse blanket. Good enough.

"It has been a pretty stressful day. I think I do need to relax a little." She reached for the waist of her jeans and undid the top button.

She heard the breath Justus expelled.

Out of the corner of her eye, she saw the smile cross Dakota's lips.

"I know just the thing." He followed her to the hay where she sat on the edge and unzipped the fly of her pants. "I know it's a little cold in here, so you better leave your sweater on. But these, have to go." She squealed again as he grabbed the legs of her jeans and pulled them off, tugging them over her boots. "And these, too."

He slipped his fingers beneath the elastic of her panties and they followed the path her pants had taken.

She resisted the urge to cover her nakedness as the two cowboys' eyes bored into her. "Dakota. What if someone comes?" she asked.

"Lock the door, Justus."

"Uh, the lock's on the outside, Dakota."

"Oh, yeah. Guess we'll have to risk it then." Dakota smiled, obviously teasing her. "No one's going to come out here. Blue's away. Mrs. Jones will be happily watching television in her room by now. Besides, in about a minute, you won't be able to think of anything besides what I'm doing to you." Dakota got on his knees and pushed her legs wide, leaving his hands braced between her spread thighs. "Damn, you're beautiful. Come look, Justus."

Justus, rooted to the floor nearby, finally moved. He took one step closer, focused solely on her pelvis, bare before him. "Damn. That is pretty." Then he raised his gaze to her face. "But then every single inch of you is."

He was so adorable, she would have smiled if she weren't so nervous. "Justus?"

"Yeah." He licked his lower lip with the tip of his tongue.

"Kiss me?" Nerves threatening to overtake her, she needed Justus to anchor her. The feel of his lips. His strong arms around her.

"My pleasure." He kneeled on the blanket next to her. His warm hands cupped her face and then his lips met hers.

She melted into his kiss, trying not to be freaked out that just below them Dakota still kneeled, slowly stroking his fingertips up and down the skin on the inside of her thighs. Each pass he made brought him a little closer to what she knew would be his final destination. Each time he almost reached it but didn't, she twitched, craving his touch.

At the same time, Justus tangled his hand in her hair and angled his head. He pushed his tongue between her lips and she met it.

His tongue stroked hers until she moaned. Then Dakota's fingers parted her other lips and her breath caught in her throat.

He touched her gently, playing lightly over the tight bundle of nerves, clenched and ready. Then the warmth of his tongue replaced his fingers and she shuddered. He latched on to her and sucked hard, bringing her hips up as she sought more.

Between Justus's claim on her mouth and Dakota's possession of her core, Melody gasped for breath. She was going to come and soon. What was it about these men that had her poised on the edge so quickly, when her last boyfriend had rarely done it to her, no matter how much he tried and how long he worked?

Her hips rocked against Dakota's mouth. Her sounds of pleasure were swallowed by Justus, until he pulled back.

With his eyes glazed, he held her tight and watched Dakota's head bob between her thighs. Melody bit her lip to control the cries. She threw her head back as the orgasm tore through her. She wanted more. She wanted them.

She was still throbbing, Dakota still working her to the point of pain, when she pawed at Justus's belt buckle. "Open it. Open your pants."

His eyes opened wide but he didn't question. He unfastened his buckle, unzipped his pants and had his thick erection out and in his hand in no time. She leaned forward and slid her mouth over the top. It was like hard steel covered in silk as she drew him deep into her throat.

The feel of Dakota's mouth disappeared but she didn't mind. She needed a break for a bit and she needed to concentrate as Justus held her head and rocked into her mouth. She tasted pre-come. His speed increased and she knew he was close. Sucking him in hard, she reached beneath and grabbed his balls, sending his hips thrusting forward.

"Melody. I want you." Dakota's breath was against her ear again. His suggestion had her insides clenching, begging to be filled.

She pulled off Justus just long enough to say, "Yes."

Seconds later, she felt Dakota between her thighs again. He parted her with his fingers, and then she was breeched by him, thick and hard. He slid inside her, slow but firm.

Long-awaited satisfaction had her sighing against Justus's cock. She wanted this. She needed this. Spreading her legs wider, she braced her feet on the hay bale, lifted her hips and hoped he'd take the invitation to slide deeper.

He did. Dakota plunged in. With his hands braced on her hips, he pumped inside her, hard and fast.

One look at Justus showed her he was watching as Dakota pistoned into her. The expression on his face was a mixture of lust and amazement.

She scraped her teeth down his length and his focus returned to her, where it stayed. His eyes narrowing, he grabbed her head and thrust into her mouth faster, until his eyes squeezed closed and she felt his balls draw up and tighten.

With a shout he came, sending hot bursts into her mouth.

"Get yourself hard again." Dakota's voice sounded tight through his clenched teeth.

Still panting and barely out of her mouth, Justus nodded. He didn't ask why. Neither did Melody. She knew. Dakota wanted Justus to make love to her too.

Both or none at all.

She squeezed her eyes shut. Both. Yes. She wanted that.

63

So strange, but so good. Her body tightened and gripped Dakota as he thrust into her, his rhythm feeling like he was nearing the end. Then he held deep and throbbed, coming deep inside her.

Only then did the thought hit Melody. It was enough to slam her with a wave of panic. Her eyes flew open just as he pulled out and she saw the condom. He rolled it off and threw it into the trash as she breathed with relief.

Thank God he'd been thinking because she sure hadn't been.

Dakota reached into his pocket and handed a foil packet to Justus, then moved to sit behind her on the hay bale. "Lean back against me, darlin'."

As Justus, hard again, rolled the latex over himself, Dakota reclined on the bale and leaned against the wall. He lifted her onto his lap so her back was cradled against his chest. With his hands looped behind each of her knees, he pulled her legs toward her while spreading her wide for Justus. "I've dreamed of doing this just like this. Holding you while he takes you."

Her heart pounded. All that came out was a moan as he nodded to Justus, who stepped closer and angled his tip at her entrance. Justus's eyes focused on her face as he pushed forward, nudging slowly into her.

Dakota leaned low again, his breath tickling her ear. "You know what else I've dreamed of?"

She swallowed hard, not sure she could talk. Between Dakota's voice and Justus's eyes, she was lost, transfixed, totally under their spell. She'd do anything and everything they asked, gladly. Repeatedly. Wantonly.

Melody managed to shake her head.

"I want Justus to hold you like this for me, while I take you *here*." Dakota maneuvered one hand to her tight hole. He circled it slowly then pushed just the very tip of his finger against her and held it there.

Justus's stroke faltered as he saw what Dakota was doing. His eyes narrowed as his lips parted and he began to breath through his mouth.

Dakota drew her earlobe between his teeth, then released it. "I'll be gentle and patient. I promise. Just like I was with the heifer. Slow. Easy. First I'll lube up my finger really good and just hold it here until you get used to the feel of me in you. Want me to show you?"

Justus, who must have heard the question, paused, holding still, watching her face, waiting for the answer.

She nodded.

Dakota glanced up. "Justus, would you grab the lube?"

He nodded his head, but didn't speak. Melody had a feeling Justus didn't trust his voice any more than she trusted her own. He handed the tube to Dakota, who spread a generous amount on his finger. Then the slippery digit was back, slipping easily inside her just the tiniest bit. He did as he'd promised, just holding it there until she got used to the invasion. Then he started moving in and out ever so slightly.

"Once you're used to this, I'd add a second finger. Just like that." Dakota pushed a second finger into her and held it there, again, just as he said he would. She felt stretched at first, until the uncomfortable feeling subsided. Only then did Dakota move his fingers deeper.

Justus let out a shaky breath and licked his lips again. "Do you want me to wait?"

"Nope. Go ahead. I want her to feel both at once."

Justus pushed in, but slowly as he tried to watch Dakota's progress while sliding into her.

"I can go a little deeper, I think." Dakota did as he described, then scissored his fingers, spreading them wide inside her. "How's that? All right?"

She couldn't breathe, forget about talk, but she managed to say, "Yes."

Dakota's fingers stroked in and out of her. "You want us to make you come again?"

"Yes."

Dakota moved his other hand and front and pressed on her tight bundle of nerves. She nearly lurched off his lap.

"Mm. Justus inside you. Me rubbing you. Is that nice?"

"Yes." Her muscles tightened.

"If I slid into you now, you'd be totally filled. I bet that would feel good. Don't you think so?" His voice was like thick honey, washing over her. Making her want more. Want everything he could give her.

Her heart pounded so hard it nearly made her pass out. "Yes."

"I think I'm gonna try it. Just a little. Ever so gently. We'll see how it feels. Okay?"

Melody nodded.

Justus, looking as if he was about to pass out, stopped his stroke. He pulled out and waited while Dakota managed to lube himself while she sat in his lap. He lifted her hips in both hands and aligned her rear entrance over his tip, then slowly let her weight push her down onto him. She drew in a sharp breath and he stopped her descent.

"Just breathe and relax. I won't move. No more until you're ready." Dakota's words came from close behind her ear. "Justus. Rub her a little bit. Yeah, just like that. Go on, you can slide in again."

Dakota was in charge and both she and Justus did as he said. "Close your eyes, Melody. Feel Justus inside you? Feel him working you? That must feel good."

Her eyes closed, she nodded.

Justus changed his angle a bit, hitting a spot inside that sent chills straight through her. She opened her mouth and dragged in a ragged breath.

Dakota pressed her lower over him and she felt the painful stretch. A reflex made her bear down on her muscles and push against him. As she did, he slid in, until she felt the relief of the wide head of him slipping past the tight muscles to rest deeper inside.

"Okay?" Dakota asked.

"Yes."

He pushed deeper. "Melody, I'm all the way inside you."

Dakota pressed his hand low over her stomach. Justus

groaned and Dakota let out a laugh. "Justus, I can feel you."

"I feel you too. Not real sure how to feel about that." Justus panted out a laugh as he stroked into her.

"Yeah, me either. But I do know I wanna make her come."

"Be my guest." Justus moved his hand and it was replaced by Dakota's.

He went to work circling her hard, first one direction, and then the other. Her hips tipped forward toward his touch. He took advantage of the move to rock in and out of her ass.

"Oh God," Justus groaned.

"He can feel every move I make and I can feel him, we're that close inside of you. Does that get you hot, Melody?" As her muscles coiled, on the brink of release, Dakota kept crooning softly in her ear.

She gasped. Her only answer was a cry as her body spasmed, coming around them.

"Holy shit," Justus cursed as her body gripped his.

Even Dakota stopped talking and drew in a sharp breath.

The more her muscles clenched the two men inside her, the stronger the orgasm seemed to get.

Justus and Dakota moved in time with her spasms until she heard them both, Dakota first, followed almost immediately by Justus, groan with their own releases.

The speed of Dakota's finger slowed until there was only pressure, which slowed her orgasm. His steady touch kept her right there on the edge, pulsing with aftershocks. He pressed down a bit and her body gave another throb.

Dakota did it again with the same result. "I could do this all night."

"You ain't kidding." Justus, his head hanging and his brows drawn down low, continued to breathe heavily. He hadn't pulled out. Neither did Dakota. Softer, smaller, they still both filled her.

Dakota pressed one more time. "Next time, I want you totally naked."

Justus moaned his agreement.

Next time. She couldn't even accuse him of being presumptuous. Not when her body still clenched both of their cocks inside her. Not when she was imagining being pressed between their nude bodies.

"I'm gonna have to pull out soon." Justus pressed his slackening length deeper as he began to slip out.

Dakota nodded. "It's okay. Fun time's over for now anyway." He tilted a chin toward the heifer, which Melody had totally forgotten about. She was half lying down, two legs protruding from within her.

Justus took a step back. He threw the condom away, zipped up his jeans and fastened his belt while keeping his gaze on the calf and heifer. "Sorry, Melody. We have to watch and make sure its hips and shoulders don't get stuck."

"Mm, the last thing in the world I want is for you to get up, but he's right." Dakota still didn't release his hold from around her waist or on her sensitive core. "One quick kiss?"

Still buried in her and he was seriously asking if he could kiss her? Dakota had to be one of the most complicated men she'd ever met. "Sure."

"Good." He grinned. Then his mouth covered her lips. His tongue met hers, even as he thrust his hips forward to press, semi-hard, into her. He broke away on a groan. "Damn, you feel too good and if I don't pull out of you right now, I'm not going to want to. You feel okay? I didn't hurt you?"

"No, I'm fine." A little freaked out because things were so very strange, but fine.

"Good. Now up you go." Dakota lifted her like she weighed nothing, slipping out of her as he did. "There's a sink, soap and paper towels to clean up in here, but no toilet. One of us can take you to the bunkhouse if you want."

He was already moving toward the sink himself, where he wet paper towels and wiped the lube off his cock, and then he washed his hands again.

She felt slippery. This part wasn't exactly romantic. In fact, it was just plain embarrassing.

"Um, I think I'm going to go home." Melody reached for her underwear and jeans.

Justus turned. "No. Don't go. We didn't even get to eat yet. Come on. I'll bring you to the room Dakota and I share in the bunkhouse There's a nice bathroom with hot water and a shower and everything. You can get yourself together, then come back and we'll have hot stew and biscuits."

"But the calf—"

Dakota, dressed again, glanced at her, "—is going to be a while."

Melody frowned. "But its legs are out."

"Yup, but she could be like that for another hour. Easy."

Melody cringed. The whole thing was as fascinating as it was disgusting, and yet the two cowboys didn't blink an eye at the gross stuff happening right before them. Just like they didn't make an issue out of the reality that after what they'd done she'd have to clean herself up before lube, semen and possibly other things she'd rather not think about eventually would slip out of her.

Her jeans in her hands as she stepped into them, she nodded. "Okay. I'll just go clean up in your bathroom quick and then come back."

Justus grinned. "That would make me very happy. I want you to see the calf. You're going to love it. The mother licks it until it's all clean and then it walks, all on its own. It's pretty amazing."

He was pretty amazing.

She smiled. "I'd love to see. Thanks."

CHAPTER SEVEN

"Why are you awake?" Dakota squinted at Justus from his bed across the room.

"I can't sleep." Sitting up on the edge of his mattress, Justus ran his hands over his face and hair. The grey light of predawn was just beginning to filter through the window of the bunkhouse.

Dakota groaned and flung his forearm over his eyes. "We only got to bed a few hours ago."

"And now it's time to get up." Justus cocked a brow.

Just because they were up half the night waiting on that calf to be born—along with doing other things with Melody—didn't mean the rest of their work could be ignored. But work wasn't what had robbed Justus of sleeping in this morning. Thoughts of Melody were responsible for that.

"Bullshit. Mrs. Jones knows we likely didn't get to bed until after midnight. She'll hold breakfast for us, and none of those horses are gonna die if we make them wait an hour or two for their feed." With a sigh filled with resignation, Dakota sat up and propped himself against the headboard. "What's the real problem with you?"

Justus debated whether to say anything or not. Dakota was

not only his best friend, he was the only other person on earth he could talk to about this.

"Melody," Justus said only her name. That would be enough. Dakota, having been there since the very beginning, knew all the many memories and emotions those three syllables held for him—for them both.

Dakota blew out a breath. "I should have known you couldn't handle this."

Justus frowned. "Handle what?"

"This." Dakota made a hand gesture to indicate the two of them. "You and me and her."

"Well, you're wrong. I'm fine with *this*." Scowling, Justus repeated Dakota's hand gesture. "I'm absolutely perfectly fine with you and me and her."

In fact, Justus had liked it, a little too much. He was going to surely burn in hell, but watching Dakota hold Melody while he slid into her last night, then feeling Dakota slide inside her too, had made Justus harder than he'd ever been in his life.

What that said about him, he didn't want to think about too closely.

Justus had spent half the time he should have been sleeping hard as a rock with anticipation of the next time they could all be together again. All he could think about was that maybe he could be the one to slide into her ass this time. Then he'd feel Dakota inside her too, rubbing against him.

That scared the shit out of him. What the hell was that about? Was he gay?

Justus eyed Dakota, who was still looking at him unhappily. He loved the guy like a brother. Sometimes they bickered like siblings too. He couldn't imagine a life without Dakota a part of it, but that was it. Justus didn't get aroused by Dakota—unless he pictured Dakota sliding into Melody as Justus held her in between them.

Crap.

"You don't look fine at all," Dakota said as his brows rose.

Justus let out a huff of air. "I like her. A lot."

"I know. You always have." Dakota did know. He might be the only person who could appreciate how much Justus liked Melody.

"I'm worried." Justus glanced at Dakota. Might as well get it all out in the open. "Where's this thing with all of us going to go?"

Dakota shrugged. "I guess that depends on if she gets this job or not."

That was part of Justus's concern, but not all of it. It might actually be a blessing if she did have to leave town again because she didn't get the teaching job.

The alternative was even more painful—her staying in town and his having to give her up because there was no way the three of them could be together. Not in public. Not like a real girlfriend and boyfriend.

Sure, the three of them could secretly continue to have sex. Yes, they could go out in public as three old friends, but Justus wanted a real girlfriend. He wanted to hold hands in the street. Go to a movie and make out in the back row in the dark. Attend the church picnic and share a blanket with her—only in this particular scenario Dakota would be there with them too.

The people in this small town would be appalled if they even suspected the two of them shared her.

Then there was their job to consider. If they were just some unknown ranchers out working their own herd and the scandal hit, that would be bad enough. But like it or not, the Maverick ranch and Maverick Western were tied together.

A huge company like Maverick Western, which had built its reputation and customers worldwide over the past hundred years selling a wholesome western lifestyle, couldn't have this kind of thing attached to it.

Blue would be forced to fire them both as an example. Then he and Dakota would be jobless and homeless. They'd have to find a place to live and look for another job, which would be near to impossible to get in this area. Or move away where no one had ever heard of them and hope that Blue would give them a good referral so they could get another job.

Justus's stomach began to twist as he pictured being unemployed and ruined.

"If you don't say something soon, I'm gonna fall asleep." Dakota leaned back and stared at the ceiling.

"I'm good. You're right. We need to wait and see what happens with her job. Go back to sleep." Justus knew he wouldn't be able to sleep well again, not for a long time, but there was no need for both of them to suffer.

With a sigh, Dakota hoisted himself off the pillow and swung his legs over the edge of the mattress. "Too late now. I'm awake. Might as well get up. Besides, Blue's flying home today and I wanna make sure that trashcan in the calving shed is emptied before he gets back and sees anything in there he shouldn't be seeing."

Justus remembered the two used condoms and wrappers that were probably right on top of the paper towels and rubber gloves and other garbage. Not to mention the tube of veterinary lube that was most likely still on top of the bales of hay instead of back in the metal medical box where it belonged.

His face heated. So many little things could expose what the three of them were doing together, so many details they had to remember to handle to protect her and the Mavericks, all so Justus could have a few hours of stolen pleasure.

Was it all worth the risk to so many? He knew the answer, he just didn't like it.

Justus stood. "I'll swing by the calving shed, check on the heifer and calf and empty the trash while I'm there. I'll meet you inside at breakfast."

He glanced at Dakota. They knew each other too well. Dakota would know something was still bothering him.

Eventually they'd have to talk about it, but luckily, for now anyway, all Dakota did was stare at him through narrowed eyes before he nodded. "All right. See you in a few."

~ * ~

Justus walked into the calving shed and the memories of last night had him stumbling to a halt just inside the doorway. He stared at the stacked hay bales where he'd stood between Melody's legs and plunged into her for the first time while Dakota spread her wide for him.

He swallowed hard, almost able to still feel how tight and hot she'd been. Even tighter once Dakota had slid inside her too.

A shiver ran down Justus's spine as visceral memories of her muscles gripping him had parts of him twitching. His face burning, he strode toward the bales and grabbed the tube of lube.

The cap was missing. Justus dropped to his knees and had to search the floor. He finally found it amid the loose pieces of hay the night's activities had knocked off the bale.

Even as shame filled him, he couldn't hold the tube without imagining lubing up his fingers as well as his length and sliding into Melody. And the sick part was that as he pictured doing it, Dakota was there too, right alongside him sharing everything with her.

The two of them together, filling her completely.

He wanted that. He wanted her. All three of them together was hot as hell, but it was an impossible situation.

Justus couldn't even imagine giving up Melody, but the way things were, how could he keep her? This wasn't New York or Los Angeles. They weren't rich or . . . or Mormon or whatever religion that was in the TV show with all the wives and one husband. These kind of things only happened on television, right?

Sure, Justus knew things happened.

On the rodeo circuit after a party and a few too many beers all sorts of crazy, sexual stuff happened. Not to him, of course, but to guys he knew. But that was a drunken one-night thing and this wasn't like that.

People—average, boring people like him anyway—didn't really stay together as a threesome on a long-term basis. At least he didn't know of any if they did.

Justus knew what he had to do. He had to enjoy her now while he had her and then let her go. It was the only way.

He couldn't have her without Dakota, they'd made a pact and he meant to stick with it, but he couldn't keep her with both of them and not make them all social pariahs. So what he'd do is hope she didn't get the job, while praying she got a job somewhere because she needed one.

Then it would be taken out of his hands. She'd move away and it would be done.

His stomach fell at the thought, but it would be the best thing for them all in the long run. She'd leave at the end of the week and he and Dakota would get on with their lives.

That didn't mean they couldn't enjoy being with her every moment they could while she was still here though.

After he checked on the calf, he'd go inside and tell Dakota they needed to call Melody later today and make plans to see her again as soon as possible.

It would hurt like hell, letting her go after spending even more time with her, but he wasn't willing to sacrifice what little time they had left. He'd deal with the loss later.

Resolved, Justus turned to the heifer and calf. They needed more water. He grabbed a bucket and headed for the sink and let the comfortable familiarity of the tasks he'd performed for years lull his mind into a peaceful numbness.

CHAPTER EIGHT

"Blue, how the hell—"

"I got the last flight out of New York last night." Dakota's boss strode into the dining room and dropped the duffle bag in his hand on the floor.

Dakota frowned. Blue hadn't been scheduled to arrive until this afternoon. "You didn't have to. Justus called and told you it went just fine last night."

"I know but it was crazy for me to be away at the start of calving season anyway. I needed to be here. Now I am." He glanced at the table. There was a place set for Dakota and for Justus with a platter covered in hash browns and bacon in the middle. "God, I need some coffee."

"I'll go tell Mrs. Jones you're here." Dakota stood and headed for the kitchen, thinking it was a damn good thing Blue hadn't managed to get a flight any earlier.

The image of him and Justus both being balls deep inside Melody when they were supposed to be keeping an eye on the heifer hit him.

He couldn't even imagine what would have happened if Blue had walked into the calving shed then.

Well, maybe he could imagine. He and Justus would be

looking for another job. Not to mention Melody would have been so embarrassed she likely never would have talked to either of them again.

But that hadn't happened and Dakota only worried when there was something real to worry about. They hadn't gotten caught. Justus was disposing of the evidence at that very moment and all was well.

He found Mrs. Jones in the kitchen frying eggs. "Blue's back early."

Her graying brows rose high. "A little notice would have been nice."

"He was worried about the heifer so he got an earlier flight."

She didn't look convinced. "Well, he still could've called. Grab me three more eggs out of the fridge."

"Sure thing." Dakota did as asked and decided it would be wise if he just grabbed a coffee mug and filled it for Blue himself, since Mrs. Jones was both busy and cranky.

He should probably take in a plate, fork and napkin for Blue, too. That would win points with Mrs. Jones that Dakota might need later on.

He carried the steaming hot, black coffee and the place setting for Blue back to the dining room and found Justus already there.

Good, the shed must be all straightened out. No one would be the wiser.

"How are they doing?" Dakota sat while questioning Justus.

"Good. Fine. I gave them fresh water." Justus glanced up quickly before concentrating solely on the plate in front of him. He reached out and piled it high with bacon and hash browns.

Justus never was good at hiding stuff. He looked completely guilty. Oh well. Good thing Dakota was good at this kind of shit. He came up with a topic to deflect the attention off Justus. "So, Blue. I thought Miss Casey was coming back with you from New York?"

"She kept the original flight. She's got some stuff to tie up at the office this morning . . . Uh, at least I think I heard her say that at the, uh, meeting. She'll be here later this evening . . . You know, because she wanted to get some photos of the calving. For the website and that blog she started." Blue avoided meeting Dakota's gaze and stared into his coffee mug.

He might try and pretend he hadn't spent the past week in the bed of Maverick Western's Director of Marketing in New York, but they all knew better.

Blue was as bad as Justus at hiding things. They both sat at the breakfast table looking guilty as sin. Dakota smothered a smile.

Mrs. Jones came in carrying a platter full of fried eggs and broke the tension, to Justus and Blue's great relief, judging by their expressions. Amateurs.

The rest of breakfast went off without a hitch. They talked a little bit about what had been happening on the ranch since Blue'd been away.

As long as there was ranch business to concern him, Blue would never look too closely at anything else. Dakota didn't know why Justus continued to act so nervous, even as they all walked into the calving shed together.

Justus should just relax. They weren't going to get caught for what had happened last night.

Or maybe they were.

"What the *hell* are those?" Blue had no problem making eye contact now as he stood over the trash bin and glared at first Justus and then Dakota.

Dakota glanced down and saw what Blue had. Justus had forgotten to empty the trash and two very used condoms lay right on top in plain view.

"Shit," Justus blanched and mumbled the curse under his breath.

"I thought you emptied that." Dakota kept his voice as low as he could so only Justus would hear him.

"I saw they needed water. I got distracted and I guess I

forgot." The panic on Justus's face would have been funny if the situation weren't so screwed up.

Blue's chin dropped low as he squeezed his eyes shut. Dakota knew him well enough to know that was not a good sign. Yelling he could handle, but a silent Blue was bad. Real bad.

Finally he opened his eyes and blew out a breath. Blue looked from one to another. "All right. Look. I know you two are close, that you've been together pretty much forever. I'm not gonna judge you. If you two wanna live your lives together, fine. But there's gonna be some rules. I don't wanna see it. I don't wanna see any evidence of it. You two can have your time alone together when I'm not around. And this between you two better not have happened when you were supposed to be tending to that heifer."

As Blue's words sunk in slowly, Dakota eyes popped open wide. "Holy crap. No, Blue, it's not like that."

Justus, still wearing a stricken expression, looked at Dakota. "Like what?"

"He thinks you and I..." Dakota pointed at the trashcan. "That you and I were using those on each other."

Justus's mouth dropped open. "Aw, jeez. No. Blue. No."

That wasn't real articulate so Dakota decided to elaborate, and apologize, and lie. Sometimes extreme messes required all that.

"Justus and I had a couple of girls in here last night." When Justus swung his surprised gaze to Dakota at that fib, he figured he better start talking faster. "We know it's wrong, but we knew the calf was gonna take a long time and we'd have nothing to do but sit around and wait for hours, so we thought we could impress these two girls if they saw us working. If you wanna fire us, I'll understand. It was wrong and I'm sorry. We both are."

"That was damn irresponsible of you two." Blue sounded pissed, but Dakota could still see his relief. Blue was old-fashioned. He'd be so happy that he didn't have to picture the two of them doing each other in the bedroom next to his in the bunkhouse they might just get away with this.

Dakota nodded. "I know it was. I'm sorry, Blue."

"I'm sorry, too. It won't happen again. I promise." Justus finally got himself together enough to apologize as well.

"See that it doesn't. Now empty that damn trash and go check on the herd."

"Yes, sir." Dakota grabbed the bin and with a glance at Justus, headed for the door.

~ * ~

"That was close," Justus said as he glanced at Dakota on their way out to the herd in the pasture.

"No kidding." Dakota let out a snort. "Too close."

"I'm sorry. It's all my fault."

"Don't worry about it." Dakota shook his head and trudged forward.

"But if I hadn't forgotten—"

"It's fine. It's done. He's okay with it. He's not happy, but I don't think we're going to get fired over it, so it's fine."

Justus let out a sigh. "Thank you."

"For what?"

"For coming up with that lie about the two girls and protecting Melody."

"No problem."

Justus stayed quiet for the rest of the walk until Dakota finally turned to look him. "What's wrong? Why do you look so miserable? I told you everything is fine."

"Because we can't do this anymore."

"Sure we can. We just have to be more careful."

Justus came to a dead stop. "I'm not talking about just the rest of the week while she's visiting her grandparents. I mean if she does get the job here, we can't continue to do this. Eventually we'll get caught and all of our lives will be ruined."

"Maybe not. Blue was willing to accept you and I were gay as long as he didn't see it. Surely that means he'd accept that we're straight but are both with the same girl. Right?"

Justus screwed up his face. "Yeah, well, it's not just Blue we have to worry about. It's everybody else."

Dakota had never seen Justus look so miserable. He had to do something to fix it. "Then I'll bow out."

"What?" Justus's blond brows knit together.

"You and Melody can be together. Without me."

"No." Justus shook his head. "Our agreement—"

"We fulfilled our agreement. We were both with her. She didn't break up our friendship. She didn't choose one of us over the other. We're not fighting over her, I'm simply bowing out."

"Why? You don't like her?" Justus's voice rose.

"Of course, I like her." Dakota let out a short laugh at the understatement. "I like her a lot, but I won't die without her. I'm not so sure about you."

Justus frowned. "That's not true."

"Don't look so insulted. I'm just saying you two might have something real and I'm not going to stand in your way."

"You're not standing in my way."

"Justus, this is a gift. It's what you've always wanted. Accept it and be grateful." Dakota turned and started walking. He expected Justus to run up behind him and say something. He didn't.

Out of the corner of his eye, Dakota saw Justus pause and pull out his cell phone. He was probably calling Melody to tell her the good news that the two of them could be together without him.

That was fine. Good. Exactly what he'd wanted. Dakota let out a sigh and kept walking.

"Dakota! Hold up."

He stopped walking as Justus jogged toward him. There was a deep frown creasing his brow. "Melody texted me."

Dakota waited. "And?"

Justus held the phone out toward him and Dakota read the text. *I didn't get the job.*

He blew out a long slow breath. "I'm sorry, Justus. I know you wanted her to stick around."

Justus shook his head. "No, I'm sorry for her sake because she needed that job, but it's better in the long run, I think.

She's smart. She'll find a job in the city, I'm sure. This way neither one of us is with her. It's better."

"Justus, I told you I'm fine with it—"

"I heard you the first time. Look, I'm going to text her back and tell her we want to see her again tonight. Both of us." Justus accentuated the word *both*. "You okay with that?"

Dakota smiled. Justus was obviously sticking to their pact. Both of them would be with her or neither of them would. "Yeah, I'm okay with that. She's probably going to need the cheering up."

"That's what I figured. Where are we going to take her though?" Justus glanced back at the calving shed. "We can't bring her back here."

"No, definitely not. If no calves are coming and we can get away for a few hours tonight, I say we head to that hotel on the highway. We both have money saved up, so paying for it won't be a problem." Dakota liked the idea of having Melody totally naked between them in an actual bed.

Plenty of room and privacy. A whole night would be better, but whatever time they could steal would do.

"All right. I'll ask her. Unless you want to ask." Justus held his phone out toward him again.

Even though Dakota had essentially backed out of this and given Justus freedom to pursue Melody on his own, Justus was still making sure Dakota was included equally in anything that happened with her.

That was Justus. Good and loyal, right down to the bone.

Dakota shook his head and pushed the phone back toward Justus. "No, it's fine. You can ask her, but make sure you tell her I'm very sorry about her not getting the job."

"I will," Justus said. "And we can both tell her again tonight, in person."

"Yes, we will."

That's not all they'd be doing in person.

Yeah, Dakota was perfectly willing to bow out gracefully and let his best friend be alone with the girl he'd been in love with since fifth grade, but as long as Justus still invited

Dakota to join them, he'd be a fool to say no.

Dakota's mama didn't raise no fool.

They'd both do a whole lot more to console her than just tell her they were sorry if Dakota had anything to say about it.

They might be sending Melody back to her parents in the city still jobless, but she'd certainly know there were two cowboys back on the ranch who cared about her. That had to count for something.

CHAPTER NINE

Melody lay facedown on the bed in the guest room in her grandparents' house. She'd have to get up eventually. Her grandmother would wonder where she was and why she was hiding in her room all day.

She would also notice Melody's red, puffy eyes. She'd been crying on and off ever since she'd gotten the call from Mrs. Stowe that morning.

It wasn't exactly a shock the school had chosen to go with the applicant who had actual teaching experience over the unemployed graduate with the apparently useless degree in art history and no practical experience of any kind, but it still hurt.

Now what?

She forced herself to sit up and swung her feet over the edge of the bed and to the floor. Now, she'd get up and get dressed. She'd put on some makeup to cover her red nose and go meet Justus and Dakota, that's what she'd do.

Melody flipped open her phone and read that day's text-message exchange between them. They wanted to see her tonight to cheer her up.

Life still sucked, but if anything could help her forget that for even a little while, it would be Justus and Dakota.

She smiled when she reread all the messages again. At least five times throughout the day a new text had come through from Justus's phone.

Dakota and I are thinking of you.

Can't wait to see you tonight.

Cheer up. We both luv ya!

Each and every one had brought fresh tears to her eyes.

They were two of the nicest guys in the world and she'd be saying goodbye to them in a few days.

Swiping her hand over the moisture in her eyes once again, Melody got up and headed for the shower.

A little flutter started inside her stomach as she stripped naked and stepped beneath the hot stream of water. She'd be naked again soon enough and pressed between the two men.

That thought chased away her tears as nervousness combined with excitement replaced sadness.

Dakota's hands and mouth would be all over her, pushing her to places she'd never known she wanted to go. Justus would be there with kisses and loving strokes that soothed her and made her want to lean in for more.

Both of them would be inside her again.

She felt the heat in her cheeks as her face flushed when she thought of all the ways they would take her tonight.

Her muscles clenched in anticipation. She still felt deliciously sore from last night. All the sensation did was make her want more. Make her want to be filled again.

As she soaped up her hand and washed herself, inside and out, she pictured them with her here under the stream hitting her back. Justus in front of her, his soapy hands running up and down her body as he kissed her. Dakota at her back, teasing her from behind.

Her legs wrapped around Justus's hips as he held her weight in his hands and plunged inside her. Dakota stepping up and teasing elsewhere with a finger before sliding his hard length inside.

Her mind could easily conjure the feeling of her body

between these two incredible men and all the overwhelming sensations of being totally and completely taken once again.

Justus had mentioned going to a hotel and asked her if that would be all right with her.

The realization hit that they actually could all shower together there—that her fantasy could easily become reality— she closed her eyes and let the pulsing heat of the water against her skin wash away any last remnants of her depression.

Melody heard the chime sound on her cell phone and smiled. She didn't need to even reach out of the shower stall to where she'd left it on the sink to know who it would be from. Justus and Dakota were thinking of her, just as she was thinking of them.

How had she gotten so lucky? She didn't know but she'd hold on to whatever happiness she could find for as long as she could.

Less than an hour late, a little nervous, Melody drove up to the tiny hotel along the highway outside of town where they'd texted her to meet them.

Their truck was already there. Comforted by the sight, she immediately felt a surge of relief. She should have known they wouldn't leave her waiting alone in a strange place.

As if it had been choreographed, both truck doors swung open in unison and two cowboys ducked their hat-covered heads and stepped out. Her heartbeat picked up speed and an uncontrollable smile bowed her lips.

"Hey." Justus smiled. He ran a hand down her arm and leaned in through the door to plant a quick kiss on her cheek.

Dakota, always the darker of the two men in both coloring and mood, was a little more serious than Justus. He glanced around them as if looking for spies.

He palmed a hotel key in one hand as he said, "Let's get on inside."

Obviously, Dakota was worried about them being seen. She probably should have been the one worried about that. Instead, she was too busy being overwhelmed by the mere presence of the two men.

What exactly was it about them that got to her? Was it because what they did together felt as wrong as it did right?

Or was it just them—these two incredible men who by some miracle and for reasons she had yet to grasp both wanted her as much as she wanted them?

Melody couldn't think more about it because the moment the hotel room door closed with all three of them inside, Dakota's mouth covered hers.

With a moan, he pulled her closer and plunged his tongue between her lips. Then he pulled back and glanced at Justus. "You'd better take off your coat and kiss her because I'm getting naked and you're about to be way behind."

Breathless, as much from his kiss as his proclamation, Melody let her coat drop and fell easily into Justus's arms.

As her eyes drifted closed from Justus's kiss, she heard the unmistakable sound of Dakota's boots hitting the floor, one at a time. She could picture him peeling them off and dropping them, one by one. Then he'd move to stripping off his jeans.

Meanwhile, there was an amazing man right in front of her. Justus grabbed her hips and pulled them closer, pressing her against the evidence of how happy he was to be there.

Justus broke the kiss and leaned his forehead against hers. "I'm very happy to see you."

She smiled. "I'm happy to see you too." She'd be even happier after he'd shucked the clothing and she could see all of him. All of his hard muscles and sharp lines.

"I'm sorry about the job." The sincerity was evident in his tone, but she didn't want to talk about that now.

Melody pressed a finger to his lips. "Shh. No talk about that. How about the two of us get naked too. Dakota's way ahead of us."

She glanced over and sure enough, there were the tight white cheeks of Dakota's ass facing her as he bent to pull down the bedspread and sheets. She couldn't help but notice the strip of condoms and the tube of lube already on the nightstand. Her insides clenched at the sight.

Glancing up, she saw Justus staring in the same direction. He must be realizing what she had—that they'd gone from necking in the truck, to sex on a bale of hay in the barn, to spending the night together in a real bed.

The change made it feel all the more serious.

Tonight was different than the other times they'd been together. In the truck when they'd all tasted of beer and had been fully dressed, even the incredible orgasms she'd had hadn't felt serious. It had been more like the fumbling high school encounters she'd had with boys. The one big difference had been teenage boys could never know what to do to her body the way Dakota and Justus, grown men, did.

Last night in the dimly lit calving shed with the scent of cows surrounding them and half of their clothes still on, even though it had been their first time having sex together, it hadn't seemed as monumental as tonight either.

That encounter, unexpected and quick, hadn't felt real.

Not like this.

Here there was an actual bed and bright lights. Here they were getting completely naked. No hiding behind clothing. They'd all be totally exposed in front of each other.

Tonight the guys, her guys, both smelled of the same clean soap and aftershave. They'd done that for her. For this. Just as she'd showered and took extra time getting ready for them.

Dakota landed naked on the mattress with a bounce and folded his arms behind his head. "Uh, you two are way overdressed. What are you waiting for?"

His grin, and the angle of his erection as it pointed directly at the ceiling, had Melody smiling.

Next to her, Justus laughed. He glanced at her as he reached down and grabbed the hem of her shirt. "Ready?"

She nodded.

He pulled it over her head. After tossing her top onto the only chair in the small room, he reached for the button on her jeans. He leaned low and pressed his mouth close to her ear.

"Kick off your shoes." After he said the words, Justus took her earlobe between his teeth and pulled gently.

That caused a tug that ran straight through her, all the way down to the void between her legs clenching and begging to be filled.

Her eyes drifted closed and she tilted her head to the side. Justus took advantage of that and ran the flat of his tongue down her throat.

A low moan left Melody's throat and she felt him smile against her neck.

"You like that."

She nodded.

"Good." He abandoned her neck to push her jeans down her legs. She stepped out of them to stand before the two men in nothing but bra and panties.

"You're still dressed." She ran her hands over the front of his shirt.

He gazed down at her. "I guess we better do something about that."

Melody began unbuttoning his shirt until his strong lean chest and stomach were exposed. She slid the shirt down his arms and tossed it on top of hers. "You better sit down and get rid of those boots."

Justus sat and Melody kneeled in front of him. She reached down and pulled off each of his boots. There was something extremely intimate about the act.

Meanwhile, she was very aware they weren't alone. That Dakota lay on the bed, slowly stroking himself and watching her and Justus's every move.

A part of Melody was getting into being watched. She upped it another notch by opening Justus's belt buckle and sliding his zipper down. She freed him of the jeans. Still on her knees, she was eye level with his erection when it sprung up after being released from the confines of his underwear.

She slid his length between her lips and Justus's eyes drifted shut. Angling her head just enough so she could see Dakota on the bed, she caught his gaze and held the eye contact as she slid Justus in and out of her mouth.

Dakota's lips parted as his eyes narrowed. Watching her the entire time, he stroked himself as she stroked Justus.

She reached a level of arousal higher than she was aware possible.

Feeling brave, Melody released Justus from her mouth and wet her finger in her mouth. His legs were spread wide as he slumped low in the chair.

It was easy enough for her to slide her slick finger back and find his tight hole. She circled it, then pressed just the tip inside.

He opened his eyes to watch her, but didn't stop her. She took that as a good sign and took him back into her mouth even as she grew bolder and pressed her finger just a tiny bit deeper.

A deep frown creased Justus's brow, but he tilted his hips and let out a moan. She glanced at Dakota and he was stroking himself faster now, biting his bottom lip, his eyes focused intently on her and Justus.

Melody worked Justus in and out of her mouth faster as she pushed inside him to her first knuckle. When she pressed the spot she'd read about online with the tip of her finger, his hips shot up, sliding him deep into her mouth. She recovered from the surprise of that and readjusted her stance, then she pressed the spot again.

With another moan, Justus grabbed both arms of the chair until his knuckles turned white. He bucked into her mouth as she felt hot bursts hit the back of her throat.

She had barely caught her breath, and had just slid her finger out of Justus's ass, when Dakota was behind her.

As she was still bent over Justus, Dakota dropped to his knees and plunged into her from behind.

Dakota held her hips tight and pounded into her. It was exactly what she'd been craving. Laying her head in Justus's lap, she sighed as she finally felt filled again.

Justus stroked her head and hair as Dakota took her in front of him.

It didn't last long. She knew it wouldn't. She'd gotten both cowboys too worked up with her little show. That made it all the better.

Dakota came hard and loud, leaning his weight against her back once the final throbbing was finished.

"I'm sorry." Dakota's words were muffled behind her as he left his head pressed against her back.

Still laying on Justus, she tilted her head to the side. "For what?"

Dakota straightened up and slid out of her before he stood and took care of the condom. "A woman should always come first."

Justus let out a laugh. "Well, in our defense, she took me by surprise."

"Are you complaining?" She shot him a look that was probably a little cocky.

"No, ma'am." Justus grinned and grabbed her around the waist. "But we both owe you now."

Justus tossed her onto the bed and crawled between her legs, spreading her thighs wide as he went. Then the heat of his tongue was on her, working her already sensitive nerve endings. Sparks of pleasure shot through Melody. She pressed closer to his mouth.

At the same time, Dakota lay across the bed and rolled her nipple between his fingers. He pressed his mouth close to her ear. "Where did you learn that little trick you did to Justus, you naughty girl?"

Her muscles clenched as Justus slid a finger inside her while continuing to tease her, but somehow she managed to answer Dakota. "The Internet."

He circled her nipple with his tongue and then lifted his head again to look at her. "You do know that I'll be expecting you to demonstrate that move on me, too, don't you?"

Breathless, she laughed. "Okay."

Looking satisfied, Dakota nodded and then pulled her already sensitive flesh between his teeth. At that moment her body coiled tight and snapped with release. Melody came hard, pressing her core against Justus's mouth at the same time Dakota's worked her nipple.

She was loud, but this was a hotel in the middle of nowhere and they were probably the only people staying here, so she didn't try to be quiet.

The guys didn't seem like they minded her volume. At least their groans made her think that.

When she could think and breathe again, she opened her eyes and gazed down at the two gorgeously naked men draped across her body. She could feel both of them were hard again, ready for more.

As crazy as it seemed after the incredible climax that had just rocked her, Melody wanted more too. She eyed the lube on the table. That would work nicely for the demonstration she owed Dakota. And at the same time, it would be very nice if Justus would kneel behind her and slide inside.

The three of them together was beginning to feel natural.

She realized how much she'd miss this when she left in a few days. That thought brought on a wave of sadness.

Melody squelched it and looked at Dakota. "Roll onto your back and bend your knees." She glanced down at Justus. "Can you grab the lube for me?"

The surprise on both cowboys' faces was enough to make her smile. Nice to know she could still shock them.

Inspired, she began to plan their activities for the rest of the night.

They hadn't seen anything yet.

CHAPTER TEN

"Miss Casey. Good to see you back again." Dakota extended his hand, but instead of shaking it, she pulled him in for a hug.

She'd always been way friendlier than he'd expected, her being from New York City and all. Maybe all that stuff about New Yorkers being nasty was bullshit, because Miss Casey didn't seem to have a mean bone in her body.

It didn't hurt that the body she had was smoking hot, but Dakota tried not to notice that now that Blue was with her.

"Dakota, it's so good to see you again." She finally released him from the hug—not that he was complaining—and took a step back.

"I thought you were due in yesterday afternoon."

She groaned. "I was. There was a snowstorm in New York. Every February we get hit with a big one and I swear it's always on the day I'm supposed to travel. They cancelled a whole bunch of flights, mine included, but I'm here now. I got in late last night. So, I hear there's a new baby."

He grinned at the excitement he saw in her expression when talking about the calf. "Yup. And in fact, we had three more born during the day today. Things are really picking up now, but those were quick deliveries, not like the last one. They're all out in the calving shed. I'll bring you out to see if you want."

"I'd love to see." The brunette held her cell phone in her hand. "I can take pictures, right? It won't bother the mothers and the babies?"

"I doubt they'll even notice. Come on. I was heading over there anyway to check on them. You can come with me." If Dakota was extra nice and helpful to Casey, maybe Blue would forget about the little incident in the calving shed with the condoms in the trash.

"Thanks. So what have I missed since I've been here last? What's happening on the Maverick ranch?"

Dakota laughed. "Not a whole lot changes around here. Same old stuff. Except for a few new trucks and some equipment, I'd bet things probably don't look too much different than they did fifty, even a hundred years ago."

"Really. That's interesting. It's pretty timely as well. Did Bonner tell you about the new project I'm working on?"

Dakota grinned at how Blue's girlfriend called him by his given name, rather than his nickname the way he and Justus did. "No, he didn't say, but then again, we didn't have a whole lotta time to talk since he got in."

They'd been busy, on top of Dakota and Justus being on his shitlist.

"I'm going to produce a book about the history of the Mavericks. The family, the ranch, the company. All of it in a big, beautiful, hardcover coffee table book with both a written history and pages of pictures showing everything. I want to include whatever old photos I can find, and then take new ones of the ranch now and of you guys working, if you're willing."

Dakota raised a brow. "Sure. I always wanted to be famous."

She laughed. "You already are. Have you seen how many girls post messages to you on the Maverick Western social networking sites?"

"Uh. No, I hadn't noticed." He cringed. "Sorry."

"It's okay, Dakota. You guys are busy. And I know how bad cell phone signal is around here and how hard it is to come by an Internet connection. I don't expect you to spend your time responding to hundreds of comments. I put an intern at the New York office on the project. You just keep texting photos of the stuff you do on the ranch to the sites and I'm happy…and so are our female customers. Believe me."

Dakota laughed. "Okay, good."

He had no problem sending in a few pictures of him and Justus working the cattle if it made Miss Casey and all those customers happy. Who was he to deprive hundreds, possibly thousands, of women of the happiness it would bring them?

Yeah, that thought wasn't making his head swell with pride too much. He had to watch it or he'd become conceited.

"I'm going to have to eventually hire someone to do the leg work for this book though. I'm already stretched too thin. I don't have time to paw through records and photos here in Colorado. I'm sure the historical society has stuff I could use. Not to mention the local town hall. Maybe even the church has some records." Casey let out a sigh and looked every bit as frustrated and stretched thin as she sounded.

It was then that an idea hit Dakota. The problems of the two women closest to him seemed to be able to be solved with one solution.

"Um, Miss Casey, would a person with a college degree in art history maybe be able to help gather all the information and photos and stuff for your book?"

Casey raised a brow. "Um, sure. I don't see why not. Anyone who's graduated from college would be good at research and information gathering. A degree in art history isn't necessary to do the job, but it wouldn't hurt. Why do you ask?"

"I know somebody, it's a girl who grew up here in town and went to school with me and Justus. She just graduated college and is looking for work."

"Hmm. A local would be good. She'd know her way around, know the people who could help us locate what we need." A smile lit her face. "I think you may have saved my sanity, Dakota. She and I would have to talk first, of course. I could guarantee her six months worth of work. Her part of the project will take at least that long. Can you have her call me? I'm here for the next week."

Casey handed him a business card with her number and email address on it and the full impact of what he'd just accomplished began to hit Dakota. If Casey hired her, Melody would be able to stay in town and Justus wouldn't have to say goodbye to her—well at least not for the next six months. They could worry about the future after that.

Excitement caused an uncontrollable smile to spread across Dakota's lips. "I surely will, Miss Casey. In fact, Justus and I were hoping to meet up with her tonight. I'll be sure to give her this."

Dakota led the way to the calving shed. As a very happy Casey began snapping photos of the new calf, he slipped through the doorway and pulled out his phone. Justus was out with the herd where there was no signal, but he could send both him and Melody the same text and Justus would get it when he was back in range.

This news was too good to wait.

Justus. Melody. I have great news! When can we all meet?

He pocketed the phone and slipped back into the shed where Miss Casey was now busy petting one of the calves, even though the heifer looked like she'd rather be left alone.

Cows and calves Dakota could handle in his sleep, which was good, because at least half of his attention was on the cell phone in his pocket waiting for the response to his text. He couldn't wait to tell them, but wait he would—at least until they were all together.

Hopefully that would be sooner rather than later.

CHAPTER ELEVEN

Justus glanced at Dakota and then at the antique grandfather clock in the corner for probably the hundredth time in the past ten minutes. "What do you think's going on in there?"

"I think Miss Casey's getting to know Melody a little better and once she realizes she's perfect for the job, like I told her she was, she'll hire her."

How could Dakota be so patient? Justus took another turn around the dining room where he'd almost paced the Maverick's carpet bare. He took another peek down the hallway toward the door of the office where Melody was meeting with Casey for her interview. "You really think she's gonna hire her?"

"I do, which is why you need to relax and sit the hell down."

When Justus finally did sit, even though it was only on the very edge of the chair, Dakota stood and moved to the chair closest to him. "Justus. Even if—when—she gets the job, remember it's only for six months. Maybe we can hope for a year, maximum, if Miss Casey gives her other stuff to do for the book."

"I know, but a lot can happen in that time."

She could find another job here locally. Miss Casey could decide she liked her work so much she hired her full-time. He could fall totally in love with her.

Hell, Justus was afraid that was already starting to happen. He couldn't think of anything but her.

Memories of last night had him walking into walls, and doing stupid shit like turning on the hose and forgetting to turn it off until long after the horse's bucket had overflowed.

But no man could have the kind of night he and Dakota had with Melody and not be affected by it.

He glanced at Dakota, still looking too damn calm considering Melody's future was going to be determined by what was happening in that room.

"I want to make sure you know, what I said before still holds true. If Melody gets this job, and if you want to be with her, I'll bow out. No fighting. No jealousy—"

"No." Justus shook his head.

He'd thought about things a lot lately and more than that, he'd actually researched their situation. Him, a cow wrangler, had actually driven until he could get a decent signal and had gotten on the Internet on his cell phone's browser.

He'd searched three-way relationships like his and Dakota's and Melody. After Melody had told them she'd learned that crazy move that had made him shoot off like a geyser on the Internet, he'd thought he'd give it a shot for this.

Boy had it been an eye-opener. Apparently they were not so unique after all, and that had inspired Justus to let this thing with them play out for a little longer.

Yeah, it might end with just him and Melody together.

Hell, it could end with neither of them with her. She could move back to the city and they'd both find girlfriends here. He didn't know.

"Justus, just think about what I—"

He didn't want to think about it. "Dakota, I like the way things are for now. Don't you?"

His best friend on Earth nodded his head. "I like it just fine. You know that."

"Then we'll let it ride and see where things go. Okay?"

"Just promise me that if in the future things change—"

"If things change, then we'll discuss it. All three of us this time, not just the two of you," Melody said as she appeared in the doorway, arms crossed over her chest. "Since I'm going to be working here for the next six months, that's how things are going to be. All three of us, together, got it?"

She cocked a brow and waited. As what she'd said sunk in, Justus knocked himself out of the shock and ran for her. With a whoop, he picked her up and spun her around. "You got the job?"

Melody smiled. "I did."

More than that, she wanted to be with him, with them both, and that was damn good news. Especially after last night in the hotel, which was very possibly the most amazing night of his life.

The three of them had made love for hours and then fallen asleep with Melody snuggled in between them until they had to sneak back to the bunkhouse, only to find, as expected, Blue wasn't there anyway because—not coincidentally—Miss Casey had arrived and was staying in the main house.

Dakota stepped up to them and smiled. "Congratulations. You deserve it."

"Thank you. I would have never got the job if you didn't suggest me for it." She shook her head.

Justus watched the exchange. It was a far cry from that night just a few days ago when Dakota and Melody had faced off in the bar. Him holding his grudge, her holding on to her façade to impress them.

Hell, it was even further from where they all were back in fifth grade when she'd caused them to pummel each other. Now, things between the three of them were like night and day from the past.

Dakota leaned in and, with Melody was still in Justus's

arms, he kissed her solid on the mouth.

When Dakota pulled back, she was smiling bigger than Justus had seen her smile since she'd been back in town.

Justus smiled just from looking at her and how happy she was. "I think we need to celebrate."

Melody nodded. "Definitely. What should we do?"

"I have a few ideas." Dakota lifted his brows suggestively.

Justus laughed. "I'm sure you do."

And he couldn't wait to find out what they were.

Want more about the folks at Maverick Ranch? Look for COWBOY BLUE, Bonner Blue Boyd and Casey's love story.

ABOUT THE AUTHOR

A top 10 *New York Times* bestseller, Cat Johnson writes the *USA Today* bestselling Hot SEALs series. Known for her creative marketing, Cat has sponsored bull riding cowboys, promoted romance using bologna and owns a collection of cowboy boots and camouflage for book signings.

Find more of Cat's contemporary romance featuring hot alpha heroes who often wear cowboy or combat boots at

CatJohnson.net

Join the mailing list at catjohnson.net/news

Made in the USA
Middletown, DE
16 March 2017